THE LAST WALTZ

THE GAZA MINUET

AND

PUTIN THE NUTCRACKER SUITE

BY

G S WILLMOTT

CONTENTS

Just Another Day in Gaza

Chapter 1

Gaza City August 1 2024

The Palestinian family were walking along Salah al Din Road intending to purchase their groceries. This was a weekly occurrence. The Saleh family consisted of Klialed the father, Hannan the mother, two boys, Ahmed, 13 and Ibrahim 16, and the daughter, Mona, 12.

Once their shopping had been completed, they decided to partake of a coffee at their favourite coffee shop. The Jooj Gallery had been a regular stop after shopping for many years.

Ibrahim excused himself from the table to go to the toilet. He never returned to the table. His family searched for the remainder of the day without success. Klialed reported his son missing the following morning. The police officer was empathetic but not confident this man would ever see his son again.

While in the amenities block at the back of the café, Ibrahim was accosted by two Hamas members of the Qassam Brigade.

'Hey boy, how old are you?'

'Sixteen. Why?'

'Do you love Gaza?'

'Of course I do. It's my home.'

'Do you hate Israel?'

'I'm not sure if you call it hate.'

'They must be destroyed. They occupy our land, and they slaughter our people.'

'Okay, but what's that got to do with me? I'm just a high school student who has an ambition to become a doctor and help my people.'

'Well, we can help you help your people right now.'

'How?'

'Join the Qassam Brigade and help eliminate Israel.'

'No, I'm happy going to school and being with my family.'

'I don't think you understand, kid. You've got no choice. You're coming with us.'

The Hamas operatives grabbed Ibrahim by his arms and dragged him to their underground lair. He was forced to climb down a steep ladder and travel along a long concrete tunnel. Finally, they entered a large room where about twenty boys about Ibrahim's age sat leaning against the walls.

For what seemed like days the boys were not informed of their fate. It was in fact one day.

Finally, a distinguished-looking man entered the room and called all to attention.

'This state will come from resistance, not negotiation. Liberation will result in statehood.

'Palestine is ours from the river to the sea and from the south to the north. There will be no concession on any inch of land.'

The boys listening to the Hamas leader were visibly moved by his words.

'We will never recognise the legitimacy of the Israeli occupation, and therefore there is no legitimacy for Israel, no matter how long it will take. We will free Jerusalem inch by inch, stone by stone. Israel has no right to occupy Jerusalem.

'You are the young warriors who will contribute to the fight against Israel and liberate our people.'

The boys were taken to a training camp where they would learn how to fire an AK47 automatic rifle and various other weapons, including rockets.

Hamas's ministries of education and interior ran the camps, referred to as 'the pioneers of liberation'. Some 13,000 students in grades 10-12 participated in the training camps the year Ibrahim graduated from the school of terror. This compared with 5,000 the previous year when the program was launched. The increase was largely due to Hamas's method of kidnapping recruits.

The corps of instructors consists mainly of active members of Hamas's security forces, and the curriculum includes weapons training, first aid, self-defence, marching exercises and 'security awareness' classes on identifying Israeli spies.

The Hamas government in Gaza celebrated the graduation of the recruits from the paramilitary camps which were geared to train high-school children to follow in the footsteps of suicide martyrs.

Hamas leaders, including the Hamas Prime Minister, attended the graduation ceremonies delivering fiery speeches denouncing Israel.

Ibrahim and other recruits

The Hamas Prime Minister added that female trainers are also on staff to oversee the training of the young women to follow in the footsteps of the female suicide operatives

Hammad, the Interior Minister, said the training was in preparation for the coming war with Israel.

'This generation is a sapling from God on Earth. It will harvest the enemies of God and be the pride of all nations,' he said.

Hamdi Shaqura, Deputy Director of Program Affairs at the Palestinian Centre for Human Rights, a Gaza-based watchdog, said that his organisation issued no statement on the training.

'To the best of my knowledge no other organisation in Gaza issued a statement either,' he told The Times of Israel.

The Hamas government in Gaza celebrated the graduation on a Monday. All the trainees of paramilitary camps were assembled. All were high-school children, who were told they were to follow in the footsteps of the suicide martyrs.

Hamas's Ministries of Education ran the camps, titled The Pioneers of Liberation. They were responsible for the camps each year.

Israeli sources with knowledge of the program said, 'The corps of instructors consists mainly of active members of Hamas's security forces, and the curriculum includes weapons training, first aid, self-defence, marching exercises and 'security awareness' classes on identifying Israeli spies.'

Hamas Grand Leader Ismail Haniyeh, Interior Minister Fathi Hammad and Education Minister Usama Mzeini attended the graduation ceremony. Each delivered fiery speeches stressing the importance of military training in developing a new generation of Palestinian combatants.

'Beware this generation,' Haniyeh said, addressing Israel. 'This is a generation which knows no fear. It is the generation of the missile, the tunnel and the suicide operations.'

The Hamas prime minister added that female trainers are also on staff 'to oversee the training of the young women to follow in the footsteps of the female suicide operatives.'

Hammad, the interior minister, said the training was in preparation for the coming war with Israel.

'This generation is a sapling from God on earth. It will harvest the enemies of God and be the pride of all nations,'

Hamdi Shaqura, deputy director of program affairs at the Palestinian Centre for Human Rights, a Gaza-based watchdog, said that his organisation issued no statement on the training.

'To the best of my knowledge no other organisation in Gaza issued a statement either,' he told The Times of Israel.

A child practises shooting at the 'Pioneers of Liberation' camp in Gaza.

Omar Dawabha, an eleventh grader who took part in the training, was quoted on the website of Hamas's Interior Ministry saying that he learned how to safeguard our rights and principles. Another student, Mohammedicalicalicalicalical Abu Nar, addressed the Al-Aqsa Mosque in Jerusalem at the graduation ceremony.

'We are the pioneers of liberation, we are coming to purify you from the Zionists,' he said.

Training to Kill

The Son of the Father

Chapter 2

While Ibrahim was being trained in using terror tactics against Israel, his family, led by his father Klialed, continued their search.

They questioned his classmates to no avail. They questioned his teachers. They too missed one of their brightest students.

One month passed and the family remained distressed. Finally Klialed decided to consult his close friend who was an active member of Hamas.

He arranged to meet Amir at the same coffee house where his son went missing.

The two men sat at a table at the back of the café hoping to be anonymous.

'Amir, I requested to meet with you in regard to my son Ibrahim.'

'Why— has he got himself in trouble?'

'No, well… I don't think so. He disappeared from the bathroom at the this very coffee shop where the family gathers after we go shopping on a Saturday morning.'

'So why come to me? I would have thought you would have reported him missing to the police.'

'We have, but you know how effective they are searching for missing persons.'

'Do you believe he has been recruited by Hamas?'

'I thought it could be a possibility.'

'Let me make some enquiries. I make no promises, but I will do my best. If it does turn out that Ibrahim has joined Hamas, you won't get him back any time soon. Hamas needs all the brave fighters it can get. We must destroy Israel and get our country back.'

'I understand, Amir, but my boy…'

The two men made their farewells.

Klialed returned to the family apartment and Amir to his underground fortress.

Two weeks later Amir contacted his good friend.

'I'm afraid I have bad and good news, Klialed. Your son has indeed joined our sacred movement.'

'Oh my God! How in Allah's name is there good news to come from that?'

'Because he is a hero ensuring Israel is destroyed.'

'I'm afraid I don't see it from your perspective, Amir. He is a sixteen-year-old boy with an ambition to become a doctor.'

'It's not the end of the world, friend. He will return to his family one day.'

'If we are lucky.'

'I will try and keep track of him and let you know of his welfare.'

'If you could the family would appreciate it.'

The two old friends made their farewells.

LIVE AS IF YOU WERE TO DIE TOMORROW

CHAPTER 3

Ibrahim and the other Hamas recruits were aware that the training was becoming more intense. This fact gave them the feeling that an attack on Israel was imminent. This also gave them all a sense of excitement and much trepidation. They knew some of them would not return; either killed in battle or captured by the enemy.

'How are you guys feeling about this whole thing? To tell you the truth I'm feeling scared. I don't particularly want to die this young. I'm still a virgin for God's sake,' said Ibrahim.

Ashan, Ibrahim's closest friend since being recruited by Hamas, agreed. He too felt great trepidation but also knew he had no choice.

Rumours started to circulate amongst the young recruits that they would soon be taking part in some sort of raid into Israel.

'I've been thinking,' Ibrahim said to Ashan. 'We should avoid the upcoming battle and live for another day.'

'And how do you propose we do that my friend?'

'Don't worry. I think I've got it covered.'

'If we were successful where would we go? Not Israel as we would end up rotting in jail.'

'Not Israel; Egypt.'

'So we just walk up to the Egyptian border guards and ask them for free passage?'

'The border is not closely patrolled. We find an isolated spot and cross over.'

'Then we find ourselves with no money and not even a water bottle. We could die in the Negev desert.'

'I stole two backpacks and water bottles and a packet of biscuits; we should also take our blankets. It's not much but it will have to do until we can get some more supplies.' Ibrahim had it all worked out.

'How are we going to purchase supplies when we have no money?'

'We have money. Don't worry.'

'How do we navigate through myriads of tunnels? We take the wrong tunnel, and we could end up slap bang in the HQ of Hamas.'

'I have a complete blueprint of all the tunnels.'

'How in the hell did you get that?'

'The last time we exited for training I noticed the plan on a desk. I took it and shoved it under my shirt.'

'Surely they will notice it missing.'

'I'm sure they all know the layout by now. They won't know it's missing.'

'I hope you are right, comrade.'

'So do I.'

'When are you planning for the great escape?'

'Tomorrow night.'

'That's not much notice... but okay.'

The two escapees had fitful sleep knowing if things didn't go to plan, they would be dead by the next day. Hamas didn't take kindly to deserters.

'Have you decided what tunnel we should take? We don't want to pop up in Israel.'

'The one that gets us on the Egypt side of the security fence,' Ibrahim explained.

'Sounds good.'

The two escapees waited until darkness before they began their daring venture.

Ibrahim had memorised the route. 'I'll leave the map behind as we go,' he told Ashan.

They slipped out of their quarters without alerting the other recruits and made their way to the Egypt tunnel.

They moved into the entrance without incident and Ibrahim instructed Ashan to lay low. They needed to listen to ascertain if there was any noise emanating from the tunnel as Hamas used it for supplies on a regular basis.

All was quiet and after waiting for fifteen minutes they began their journey to freedom.

The tunnel was one kilometre long and it took them fifteen minutes to reach the exit. Ibrahim slowly looked out. He saw nothing other than the security fence; no guards were in sight. He signalled for Ashan to follow him out.

Both escapees ran, bending over to reduce their profiles.

Once a reasonable distance from the border they resumed their normal stance.

'We made it!' said Ashan.

'Don't get too excited. We have a long journey in front of us with the Hamas guards possibly hot on our trail. It's 350 kilometres to Cairo.'

'What do we do when we finally reach there?'

'My uncle is a wealthy businessman living in an expensive suburb. He will help us get to our final destination.'

'And where might that be, Ibrahim?'

'I don't know. Maybe America or Australia… somewhere safe.'

'And how do we navigate our journey when we don't have a compass?'

'Ever since I was a kid, I've been fascinated by the stars in the night sky. My parents gave me a telescope when I was ten, and I used it every clear night. I will navigate by the stars. We need to head south. Let's go.'

The autumn in the Negev was quite mild the boys experienced temperatures of 26 degrees during the day dropping to15 at night. This made ideal conditions for their long trek.

By the third day their rations were low. It was obvious they needed to source some more food and water but they knew it would be serendipitous to discover an oasis.

Just when things were getting desperate, they sighted a camel train.

They approached the Bedouin leading the beasts and requested food and water.

He agreed and provided the boys with pita bread, dates and water for the agreed price.

Ibrahim and Ashan continued on their journey to Cairo with a refreshed sense of hope.

As they approached, Ashan again began to question their future. 'Ibrahim, have you considered that your uncle may not fund the rest of our journey?'

'I have thought of that, but I do have a contingency plan.'

Ibrahim opened his backpack and pulled out the blueprint of the Hamas tunnels.

'You told me you had left it back in the tunnel. Why did you lie to me?'

'I didn't want to worry you,' Ibrahim said. 'This will be our passport to freedom. We can sell it to the highest bidder which will probably be the USA.'

'Yes, and they will pass it on to Israel.'

'We owe Hamas nothing, Ashan. Just remember we were kidnapped and taken away from our families to become cannon fodder. I am not nor will I ever be a supporter of Hamas and what the organisation stands for and the fact you escaped with me would indicate you agree with me.'

'I suppose you're right; I just hope Hamas don't track us down and discover the blueprint. God knows what they would do to us.'

The two boys began their third day of their dangerous journey which they hoped would end in Cairo in four days' time.

They were thankful they'd brought the blankets supplied by their kidnappers as this made sleeping in the desert tolerable.

The Palestinian boys persevered for another four days and at last they could see the pyramids in the distance.

'We made it! Soon we will be with my uncle Fahad in his beautiful home,' Ibrahim said.

'Yes, but we need to be careful. Hamas has spies everywhere. I'm sure they will be looking for us.' Ashan sighed. 'I take it you know his address?'

'Oh yes, he sent all the members of our family cards for our birthdays and on the back of the envelope was his address at 16 Abul Feda Street, Zamaek.

'Okay. Let's find it although without a street map I'm not sure how.'

The boys walked through the Khan el-Khaill market, totally entranced by the stalls and numbers of people browsing the products for sale.

At last they found what they were looking for, a bookshop, which also sold city street maps.

They paid the vendor one pound and searched for a quiet spot to examine the detailed map. It didn't take them long to find the island of Zamalek.

Zamalek is an affluent district on a man-made island which is geologically a part of the west bank of the Nile River, with the bahr al-a'ma (Blind Canal) cut during the second half of the 19th Century to separate it from the west bank proper.

Ibrahim and Ashan headed for the Qasr El bridge which would take them to Zamalek Island and Ibrahim's uncle.

Eventually they located Abul Feda street where Uncle Fahad's mansion was located.

Inrahim knocked on the magnificent carved wooden front door and a tall Arabian man opened the door.

'What do you want? We don't accept beggars knocking on my master's door. Please leave.'

'Sir, I am your master's nephew. We look like beggars, but we are not. We have trekked from Gaza across the Negev; hence our shabby appearance.'

'What are your names? I will inform him of your presence. Wait here.'

'My name is Ibrahim and my friend's name is Ashan.'

The servant closed the door and located his master.

'Sir, I have two unkempt boys at the door. One of them, Ibrahim, claims to be your nephew.'

'I do have a nephew by that name, so let me see them. Bring them into my study.'

The two boys were ushered into Fahad's study.

Ibrahim and Ashan stood waiting for Uncle Fahad to enter. Ibrahim hoped his uncle would recognise him because it had been many years since they làst met.

After a twenty-minute wait, a very distinguished-looking man entered the study. He looked up and down the two boys, showing some scepticism.

'Which of you claims to be my nephew?'

'It is I, Uncle. I am Ibrahim.'

'Tell me all your family's names.'

'Klialed is my father. Hannan is my mother and my brother is Ahmed. My sister is Mona.'

'Well, it does seem you are my nephew. What brings you to Cairo and in such disarray?'

The boys told their story in detail.

Fahad was entranced. 'Well, I have no love for Hamas and what they represent. What is it you want from me other than a bath and some clean clothes?'

'We were hoping you would fund us for the next part of our journey to freedom.'

'Where do you hope to travel?'

'Either Australia or America.'

'You will require a visa for both countries. If I were you I would choose Australia. I believe you would have more opportunities there. I am friendly with the Australian Ambassador, and I will put in a good word for you. He may be able to speed up your application.'

'Does this mean you will fund our trip?'

'Of course! You are family. Your father and I are very close. I will inform him of your whereabouts when you land in Melbourne.'

'Uncle, can you recommend a hostel where we can stay until we receive our visas?'

'Even with my influence at the embassy it will take some time to have your visa approved. This can take up to nine months. I hope three months would be more likely, but even so I don't think you will be able to pay the tariff. I have a two-bedroom cottage at the back of the property where I allow guests to stay. You can reside there.'

'That's very kind of you, Uncle Fahad. We really appreciate it. May we work for you during our stay?'

Fahad smiled. 'As a matter of fact my gardener has just resigned!'

The two fugitives settled into their new abode. The cottage was well appointed with two bedrooms, a kitchen and bathroom. They cooked their own meals except for Sundays when they joined their host for a traditional Egyptian feast.

'We would have been in deep trouble if it hadn't for the generosity of you uncle,' said Ashan.

'We sure would have,' replied Ibrahim.

Fahad also organised an English language teacher so the boys would have some knowledge of the language when they arrived in Australia.

The two Palestinian boys enjoyed some of their gardening duties, particularly mowing the vast lawns on the ride on mower. They took it in turns.

What they didn't enjoy was weeding the vast gardens. Nevertheless they were eternally grateful for Uncle Fahad's hospitality.

Four months passed with no sign of the permanent residents' visas. The boys were having doubts as if they would ever receive them.

Finally they received notice that they were to attend the Australian Embassy.

Fahad arranged for his driver to take them to the embassy, where they caught the lift to the eleventh floor of the World Trade Centre. They entered the ambassador's anteroom, feeling very nervous.

'Excuse us, miss… we have an appointment with the ambassador,' ventured Ibrahim.

'Really? He doesn't normally meet with such young men. What are your names? I'll see if you are listed for a meeting with His Excellency.'

Ibrahim introduced himself and his friend.

The receptionist raised her brows. 'Well, it does seem that you have an appointment. Take a seat. I will let him know of your presence.'

The two boys waited nervously. If they were not given visas their grand plan was extinguished.

The door to the ambassador's office opened and the receptionist ushered them in.

'Well boys, Fahad tells me you have both been on quite an adventure escaping from the clutches of Hamas and crossing the Negev to get to Cairo. So you hope for freedom and a new life in Australia?'

'Yes, Your Excellency, that is our great hope,' said Ibrahim.

'Well, I'm pleased to inform you both that my government has approved your application. If you take the lift down to the tenth floor, Immigration will issue with the appropriate visas.'

'Thank you, Your Excellency.'

'Good luck. I hope it all works out for you.'

The boys returned to the mansion eager to tell Uncle Fahad the good news.

He was pleased for them. He informed them he had purchased tickets to Australia, and he gave them $5000 each to get them started in their new home.

'We can't thank you enough, Uncle. We will do everything in our power to make you proud.'

'I am sure you will. Your flight departs in three days' time. I will get my driver to take you to the airport.'

They enjoyed their last night together. A magnificent meal was consumed, and the boys had their first glass of fine French red wine.

Neither Ibrahim nor Ashan had flown before, so a new experience awaited them.

The time arrived to depart for the airport. The two boys thanked their benefactor for his hospitality and kindness and promised to email him upon their arrival and let him know of their progress in their new home.

Ibrahim and Ashan were amazed by the sheer size of the plane. Their seats were in the middle of the aircraft, which would give them with a good view.

The flight took eighteen and half hours. By the time they landed in Melbourne they were shattered as neither of them slept a wink for the entire flight.

They caught the shuttle bus to the CBD and located the youth hostel Uncle Fahad had booked from Cairo.

Melbourne was an eye opener for the two Palestinians. The city had more skyscrapers than Cairo and it was so clean!

The first day of their new life awaited them. They were both excited but fearful of what lay ahead.

ISRAEL

CHAPTER 4

History of Hamas and Israel

2000: The second intifada, or Palestinian uprising, began after riots broke out following a visit by right-wing Israeli political figure Ariel Sharon (and later prime minister) to a compound in Jerusalem venerated in Judaism, Christianity and Islam (The Temple Mount). Clashes and other violence continued until 2005, leaving hundreds dead on both sides.

Palestinian supporters of the Islamic group Hamas celebrated their victory in the Palestinian parliamentary elections during a rally in Gaza City on Jan. 27, 2006.

2006: The Palestinian militant group Hamas won elections in Gaza, leading to political strains with the more moderate Fatah party controlling the West Bank.

Israeli warplanes retaliated against rocket fire from Gaza pounding dozens of security compounds across the Hamas-ruled territory in unprecedented attacks from airstrikes.

December 2008: Israel began three weeks of attacks on Gaza after rocket barrages into Israel by Palestinian militants. The rockets are supplied by Egypt, using tunnels. More than 1,110 Palestinians and at least 13 Israelis were killed during the confrontation.

November 2012: Israel killed Hamas military chief Jabari, touching off more than a week of rocket fire from Gaza and Israeli airstrikes. At least 150 Palestinians and six Israelis were killed.

Summer 2014: Hamas militants killed three Israeli teenagers who were kidnapped near a Jewish settlement in the West Bank, prompting an Israeli military response. Hamas answered with rocket attacks from Gaza. A seven-week conflict left more than 2,200 Palestinians dead in Gaza. In Israel, 67 soldiers and six civilians were killed.

December 2017: The Trump administration recognised Jerusalem as the capital of Israel and announced that it planned to shift the US Embassy from Tel Aviv, stirring outrage from Palestinians.

2018: Protests took place in Gaza along the wall with Israel, including demonstrators hurling rocks and gasoline bombs across the barrier. Israeli troops killed more than 170 protesters over several months. In November, Israel staged a covert raid into Gaza. At least seven suspected Palestinian militants and a senior Israeli army officer were killed. From Gaza, hundreds of rockets were fired into Israel.

May 2021: After weeks of tension in Jerusalem, which led to Israeli police raiding al-Aqsa Mosque, one of the holiest sites in Islam, Hamas fired rockets towards the city for the first time in years, prompting Israel to retaliate with airstrikes. The fighting, the fiercest since at least 2014, saw thousands of rockets fired from Gaza and hundreds of airstrikes on the Palestinian territory, with more than 200 killed in Gaza and at least 10 killed in Israel.

December 2008: Israel began three weeks of attacks on Gaza after rocket barrages into Israel by Palestinian militants. More than 1,110 Palestinians and at least 13 Israelis were killed.

The **2022 Gaza–Israel clashes** lasted from 5 to 7 August 2022. The Israel Defence Forces (IDF) conducted some 147 airstrikes in Gaza and Palestinian militants fired approximately 1,100 rockets towards Israel.

October 6 2023

Israel-Hamas War, war between Israel and Palestinian militants, especially Hamas that began on October 7, 2023, when Hamas launched a land, sea, and air assault on Israel from the Gaza Strip. The October 7 attack resulted in more than 1,200 deaths, primarily Israeli citizens, making it the deadliest day for Israel since its independence. More than 240 people were taken hostage during the attack.

The next day, Israel declared itself in a state of war for the first time since the Yom Kippur War in 1973. The war began with the Israeli Defence Force (IDF) conducting air strikes on the Gaza Strip, followed weeks later by the incursion of ground troops and armoured vehicles. By November 2024 more than 43,000 Gazans, about 2 percent of the territory's population, had been killed and two-thirds of the buildings in the Gaza Strip had been damaged or destroyed.

Ethan Cohen was looking forward to his eighteenth birthday. Over fifty of his friends and family members had been invited to his party. Only his bar mitzvah surpassed this event.

Another event that didn't excite him as much was his conscription into the army. The law stated that every boy must serve thirty-two months while girls were required to serve twenty-four months.

Male conscripts in training

There was one redeeming feature about joining the IDF. His elder brother, Sam, had been conscripted twelve months before. Ethan hoped he could join his brother's unit stationed on the Israeli Lebanon border.

The day arrived when Ethan bade farewell to his family. Now only his mother and father plus his younger sister, Ruth, remained in the family home located in the Be'eri kibbutz in central Israel.

As an 18-year-old combat recruit, Ethan would go through a yearlong training process. During this process, he would perfect his physical and mental skills in order to transform into an IDF combat soldier.

His transformation started at the induction centre, where he and the other recruits received their uniforms. Officials interviewed him and he was required to complete various forms and prepared for the journey ahead. He travelled directly to the brigade-training base, where he would spend the next several months.

There he would begin basic training which turned civilians into soldiers. In basic training, he learnt the values and fundamentals of combat soldiers, including routine and military discipline, physical training, field weeks, weapons training, shooting, and the principles of the IDF. Ethan's basic training lasted approximately four months and ended with a final march.

The final march was called the Masa Kumta. Ethan, along with his comrades in arms, was required to march forty kilometres in combat gear carrying a stretcher. After completing the march Ethan received his unit beret. His unit was Givati Brigade, a combat unit with a fierce reputation.

At the end of the march, Ethan attended a swearing-in ceremony, in which he officially joined the ranks of the IDF.

Ethan Proudly donning his Brigade beret

Ethan's training didn't cease there. He would now commence his advanced training for which he was assigned a role in the brigade.

As a regular infantry brigade, the Givati Brigade undertook ongoing security operations including serving in the Territories, patrolling the borders, and manning positions in Lebanon. The brigade undertook these responsibilities just as its older sister brigades did, and also had its own infantry specialisation—marine amphibious landings.

The end of the ceremony symbolised the beginning of Ethan's advanced training. After a year, he was able to begin operational duty.

During advanced training, soldiers learn how to work together as a team, starting as the smallest group, the squad, and ending with the whole company. They put emphasis on fitness, readiness, and the proper care of military equipment. At this point, they also deepen their knowledge of different combat techniques and specialisations.

A surprise attack by a Palestinian group, Hamas, on Israel, combining gunmen breaching security barriers and a barrage of rockets fired from Gaza the attack was launched at dawn during the Jewish holiday of Simchat Torah.

Saturday's attack came 50 years and a day after Egyptian and Syrian forces launched an assault during the Jewish holiday of Yom Kippur in an effort to retrieve territory Israel had taken during a brief conflict in 1967.

Here's how the brazen assault unfolded:

At about 6:30am, Hamas fired a huge barrage of rockets into southern Israel with sirens heard as far away as Tel Aviv and Beersheba.

Hamas said it launched 5,000 rockets in an initial barrage.

Smoke billowed over residential Israeli areas and people sheltered behind buildings as sirens sounded. At least one woman was reported killed by the rockets.

'We announce the start of Operation Al-Aqsa Flood, and we announce that the first strike, which targeted enemy positions, airports, and military fortifications, exceeded 5,000 missiles and shells,' Mohammed Deif, head of the Qassam Brigades, the military wing of Hamas, said.

He died on July 13, 2024, killed by an Israeli air strike in Palestine.

Mohammed Deif

The rocket attack served as cover for an unprecedented multipronged infiltration of fighters with the Israeli military acknowledging that Palestinian fighters had crossed into Israel.

Most fighters entered through breaches in security barriers separating Gaza and Israel, but at least one Hamas soldier was filmed flying over in a powered parachute. A motorboat carrying fighters was seen heading to Zikim, an Israeli coastal town with a military base.

One video showed at least six motorcycles with fighters crossing through a hole in a metal barrier. A photograph released by Hamas showed a bulldozer tearing down a section of fence.

Several people involved in collecting and identifying the bodies of those killed in the attack reported they had seen multiple signs of sexual assault, including broken pelvises, bruises, cuts and tears, and that the victims ranged from children and teenagers to pensioners.

Video testimony of an eyewitness at the Nova music festival, shown to journalists by Israeli police, detailed the gang rape, mutilation and execution of one victim.

Videos of naked and bloodied women filmed by Hamas on the day of the attack, and photographs of bodies taken at the sites afterwards, suggest that their attackers sexually targeted women.

Few victims are thought to have survived to tell their own stories.

Their last moments are being pieced together from accounts by survivors, body-collectors, morgue staff and footage from the attack sites.

Police have privately shown journalists a single horrific testimony that they filmed of a woman who was at the Nova festival site during the attack.

She describes seeing Hamas fighters' gang rape a woman and mutilate her, before the last of her attackers shot her in the head as he continued to rape her.

GENOCIDE

No Israeli Remains Untouched

Chapter 5

Ethan's unit had been deployed in Southern Israel. Initially there was not much going on as he with his comrades patrolled the wall separating Israel and Gaza.

Nobody expected any trouble. After all, the entire wall was twelve metres high and two and a half metres thick.

The likelihood of Hamas scaling it was remote. The wall ran for 4018 metres and the Israeli citizens felt protected from a ground attack. However, Hamas seemed to have an unlimited supply of rockets.

OCTOBER 7 2023

As far as Ethan was concerned it was just another day patrolling the wall when he received a message from his commanding officer on his encrypted smart phone. The IDF had commissioned Motorola to develop the military grade phone. The contract amounted to US100,000,000; a sizeable investment but well worth it.

All thirty soldiers received the same message. Hamas had sent a large force into Israel and were killing men, women and children.

There were several points of attack. Their orders were to proceed to Be'eri, Kibbutz, which had been attacked.

Hamas militants carried out a massacre at Be'eri, an Israeli kibbutz near the Gaza Strip. Hundreds of Gazan militants and civilian looters attacked the kibbutz, killing and abducting civilians while facing resistance from armed residents.

Ethan's platoon was quite close to his family's Kibbutz.

'Quick, my family lives in Be'eri kibbutz and with God's blessing they are still alive. My brother was home on leave and I'm sure he would protect them,' said Ethan.

Ethan and three of his comrades headed for Ethan's family home. They were devastated with what they saw.

The home he had grown up in and where he had shared so many wonderful family moments had been destroyed.

The four IDF soldiers slowly entered the charred remains and they were all horrified at what they discovered.

The military took too long on the day and failed to understand the scale of the attack, sending in new recruits, including Ethan, who were ill equipped to deal with a mass assault. As the military grappled with the unfathomable situation playing out in southern Israel, the first IDF troop deployment occurred at 7:43 a.m. — over an hour into the Hamas invasion when orders were issued for all emergency forces to move south.

They began searching for Ethan's family members and eventually they found them all in his parents' bedroom. All had been shot several times and it was obvious that Ruth had been brutally raped.

Ethan fell to his knees, sobbing uncontrollably. His comrades tried to console him without success.

'Ethan, we have to find the bastards who committed this atrocity. Come on, let's go.'

Ethan and his comrades were bemused as to why?

WHAT WAS HAMAS THINKING?
AND WHAT IS IT THINKING NOW?

The size, scale, and brutality of Hamas's October 7 assault on Israel suggests that the group's aim was to fundamentally change the strategic dynamic with Israel and the Palestinian Authority, and probably in the larger region, as well.

Hamas may have believed Israel was weakened, distracted, and divided by its internal political turmoil over the past year, making this a good time to strike. Perhaps Hamas thought a surprise attack would widen political divisions in Israel, upend the Israeli government, and sap the resilience and determination of the Israeli people to prevail. Instead, it produced the unity and resolve the world is currently seeing.

Hamas may also have calculated that it had an opportunity to deal a knockout blow to the Palestinian Authority. The popularity of President Mahmoud Abbas and the Authority itself had been plummeting, and hard-line factions including Hamas cells had begun to gain traction in the West Bank by taking the fight to Israel. The October 7 attack appears to have been specifically timed to coincide with the fiftieth anniversary of the 1973 Yom Kippur war—in which Israel's apparent invulnerability was called into question by successful surprise attacks from Egyptian and Syrian armies—to catch the Jewish state off guard and deal it a major blow.

Hamas and its Axis of Resistance partners had expected that rising pro-Hamas and anti-Israeli sentiment in the Arab world would prompt Saudi Crown Prince Mohammed bin Salman bin Salman to halt efforts to openly embrace Israel for the indefinite future.

It also appears that a key aim of the attack was to derail the ongoing Saudi-Israeli talks at normalising relations between the two countries. Hamas, Hezbollah, and Iranian officials have publicly condemned the Saudi-Israeli discussions, and Hamas and Hezbollah officials also have cited the talks—which they view as a sell-out of resistance to Israel's presence in Muslim lands and a betrayal of the Palestinians—as a major motivation for Hamas's October 7 assault on Israel. These groups recognised that the establishment of normal relations between Saudi Arabia and Israel posed a strategic threat to their cause that would strengthen the pro-Western countries in the region and leave the Iran-led Axis of Resistance isolated. Iranian concern over the apparent progress of the Saudi-Israeli talks appears to have prompted the Axis of Resistance to pursue greater unity of effort to combat the threat they believe it poses. According to reporting, Hamas coordinated its attack plans with Iran and Hezbollah officials from all three organisations met in Beirut on several occasions in to discuss the operation. Hamas probably had the final call on the specifics of its operational plan and the timing of its attacks, but Iranian funding, weapons, and training over many years have been key to Hamas's increased military prowess.

Hamas leaders recognised that their attack on Israel—undoubtedly supported and endorsed by their Iranian patron— would heighten Saudi fears of Iran and desire for an eventual alliance with Israel to counter the Iranian threat. However, Hamas probably also believes that the Arab public would be cheering its attack and would rally behind Hamas in the face of the expected large-scale Palestinian civilian casualties from Israeli military operations. Hamas and its Axis of Resistance partners expected there would be a rising of pro-Hamas and anti-Israeli sentiment in the Arab world which would prompt Saudi Crown Prince Mohammed bin Salman to halt efforts to openly embrace Israel for the indefinite future.

After the October 7 attacks

Hamas probably calculated that Israel would respond with a major ground invasion to the horrific attacks the group has carried out, and most likely it has made preparations to bleed Israeli forces when they enter Gaza. Hamas probably also has placed its communications centres, fighters, and munitions among the civilian population, which will inevitably increase the number of civilian deaths. Hamas may have assessed that it can achieve a replay of previous wars with Israel, in which mounting Israeli military casualties and a rising death toll among civilians in Gaza resulted in domestic pressure in Israel and calls from the international community, including the United States, for Israel to accept a ceasefire. Hamas also planned to use the over two hundred hostages it has taken as leverage to get Israel to stop operations with Hamas still intact and able to claim victory.

However, Hamas may have misjudged both the international support it would enjoy and Israeli determination to sustain the fight. First, the sickening news of women being raped and innocent men, women, children, and elderly people being kidnapped and murdered has undermined sympathy around the world for the group's claims to be the defender of Palestinians against Israeli oppression. These acts have also bolstered support for Israel's claim that it must respond with great force to the threat Hamas poses. Even so, to avoid losing international backing for its military response, especially as its ground invasion of Gaza continued, Israel needs to show continued concern to minimise casualties and help preserve adequate humanitarian conditions for Palestinian civilians in Gaza.

Secondly, unlike in the past, the Israeli government probably will not face domestic pressure in the near-to-short term to halt its offensive. The Israeli public and all major Israeli political parties have united right now behind destroying Hamas.

A DAY IN THE LIFE

MISERABLE

CHAPTER 6

The Bakrons and al-Bareems, two families from opposite ends of Gaza, have criss-crossed the rubble-strewn territory many times during 21 months of war, in search of food and shelter from Israeli attacks.

They've sought refuge in the homes of friends and relatives, in school classrooms and in tents, moving frequently as the Israeli military has ordered civilians from one zone to another.

The Bareems, from southern Gaza, have a disabled child whom they have pushed in his wheelchair. The Bakrons, from the north, stopped wandering in May after two of their children were killed in an airstrike.

'Our story is one of displacement, loss of loved ones, hunger, humiliation and loss of hope,' said Nizar Bakron, 38, who lost his daughter Olina, 10, and son Rebhi, eight.

The families' experiences illustrate the plight of the 1.9 million Gaza residents – 90 per cent of the population – that the United Nations says have been displaced during the conflict.

'Our story is one of displacement, loss of loved ones, hunger, humiliation and loss of hope,' said Nizar Bakron, 38, who lost his daughter Olina, 10, and son Rebhi, eight.

Israel's war in Gaza has left much of the enclave in ruins and its people desperate from hunger. It was triggered by an attack by Islamist group Hamas – which governs the Strip – on Israeli border communities on 7th October, 2023, that killed some 1,200 people and took 250 hostage.

Before the war, Nizar and his wife Amal, four years his junior, had a happy life in Shejaia, a teeming district in the east of Gaza City. Their eldest Adam is 12; the youngest, Youssef, a baby.

Shejaia

Shejaia Now

'When the October 7 attack happened, I knew it wouldn't be something good for us,' Nizar said.

They left home the next day for Amal's mother's house further south in Zahra.

Five days later Israel began ordering civilians in northern Gaza to move south and, on 27th October, it launched a ground invasion.

Throughout the war Israel has issued evacuation orders in areas where it plans to conduct operations – though it has also struck elsewhere during those periods.

Israel says the orders protect civilians, but it strikes wherever it locates Hamas fighters, who hide among the population. Hamas denies using civilians as shields.

Palestinians accuse Israel of using the evacuation orders to uproot the population, which it denies.

The family left for Nuseirat, an old refugee camp in central Gaza, where they crammed into an apartment owned by Amal's relatives for five months.

Israel's bombardment was heaviest in the first months of the war. The Gaza Health Ministry, controlled by Hamas, said the death toll reached 32,845 by the end of March 2024. It has now passed 59,000 people, the ministry says.

Food and fuel were becoming very expensive, with little aid arriving. In April, Israel issued an evacuation order and the Bakrons went further south to Rafah on the border with Egypt where there was more to eat.

They loaded the car and a trailer with mattresses, clothes, kitchen equipment and a solar panel and drove 15 miles along roads lined with ruins.

In Rafah, they squeezed into a classroom of a UN school, which they shared with Nizar's two brothers and their families – about 20 people. Their savings were quickly disappearing.

Weeks later, a new Israeli evacuation order moved them to Khan Younis, a few kilometres away, and another crowded classroom.

In January, a ceasefire allowed them to move back north to Nuseirat, where the family had land. They cleared a room in a damaged building to live in.

'We thought things would get better,' Nizar said.

But, after less than two months, the ceasefire collapsed on 18th March. Two days later, Bakron's sister, her husband and two daughters were killed in an airstrike in Khan Younis.

As Israeli operations escalated, the family fled to Gaza City. They pitched a tent – the first time they had to live in one – against a building on Wehda Street, a central district.

On 25th May, as most of the family slept, Nizar was sitting outside, talking on the phone, when an airstrike hit, and the building collapsed.

He pulled away the debris; but Olina and Rebhi were dead. His wife Amal and eldest Adam were injured, and the baby Youssef's leg was broken.

Nizar does not know how they can move again. The family is in mourning and their car was damaged in the strike.

The UN estimates nearly 90 per cent of Gaza's territory is covered by Israeli evacuation orders or within Israeli militarised zones, leaving the population squeezed into two swathes of land where food is increasingly scarce. Israel says restrictions on aid are needed to prevent it being diverted to Hamas.

World Health Organization chief Tedros Adhanom Ghebreyesus said Gaza is suffering from man-made starvation.

Amal, who still has bruising on her face and wears a brace upon her arm after the attack, grieves for her two children. 'My life changed, from having everything to having nothing, after being displaced.'

Kajed al-Bareem, 32, was a teacher before the war in Bani Suheila, a town east of Khan Younis. He and his wife Samia, 27, have a two-year-old son, Samir. They lived in a pretty two-storey house.

During Israel's initial offensive, which was focused on northern Gaza, the family stayed put. But early in 2024, Israeli forces pushed into Khan Younis and the Bareems fled their home.

They learned afterwards it had been destroyed.

'I had a beautiful house which we built with our sweat and effort,' Majed said. He showed Reuters photos of the ruins.

They went to Rafah with Majed's mother, Alyah, 62 and his three sisters. The youngest, Rafah, 19, has Down Syndrome.

Days before they left Khan Younis, his eldest sister's husband was shot dead. Her son, Joud, nine, is in a wheelchair.

At first, the family stayed in a tent provided by UN aid agencies in a district called Nasr in northern Rafah.

Three months later, Israel ordered civilians to evacuate, and the family left for Mawasi, a rural area nearby where displacement camps were growing.

Although Israel's military had designated Mawasi a safe zone, it struck it throughout the summer, killing scores of people, according to local health authorities. Israel said it was targeting militants hiding in the area.

Since the two-month ceasefire ended in March the family has moved repeatedly – so often that Majed said he lost count – between Bani Suheila, Khan Younis and Mawasi.

'We fear for our lives so, as soon as they order us to leave, we do so,' he said.

Crossing Gaza's ruined streets with a wheelchair has added to the difficulty. During one journey in May, he and Joud were separated from the family. It took them four hours to travel the five miles to Mawasi along roads littered with debris.

'It was exhausting and scary because we could hear gunfire and bombing,' he said.

The family is in a tent in Mawasi. Their savings are nearly gone, and they can only rarely afford extra rations to supplement the little they get from charitable kitchens.

'We are tired of displacement. We are tired of lack of food,' said Majed's mother, Alyah.

Majed went to Bani Suheila hoping to buy some flour. A shell landed nearby, wounding him in the torso with a shrapnel fragment. It was removed in hospital but left him weak.

'I don't think anyone can bear what we are bearing,' he said. 'It has been two years of the war, hunger, killing, destruction and displacement.'

The fight for peace in Gaza is not just the work of diplomats and politicians — it's a collective effort that requires the hearts and minds of each and every one of us.

DIARY OF ETHAN COHEN

CHAPTER 7

Sunday, January 28, 10:27 p.m.

This war has continued for nearly four months, and our soldiers miss their homes and their families as I do. I will never see my family again, but we are still prepared to do whatever is needed to continue pushing towards elusive but important goals.

Even though the unity of those first few weeks has worn off, and the entire nation rallying around a common purpose has given way to political infighting and questionable leadership, countless volunteers are still cooking and baking and farming and fundraising. They haven't lost sight of what unites us. They wear their love for their fellow man on their sleeves, because they know we are in this together.

We have lost many soldiers, many from my own unit, and many have been injured. There are units whose losses seem almost too much to bear, yet our army is still filled with fearless warriors and untiring men and women who wake up day or night and head into danger.

We are all humans — and as human beings we get overwhelmed and frustrated and disillusioned, but we are still empathetic and unstoppable and motivated.

Even though I have seen many horrible things I am still as committed as ever. I still feel sad when the helicopter passing overhead is that of a medivac. I still hold my breath when we find a sign of our hostages. We still grieve when we pass the bodies of young children lying amongst the rubble.

Even though 114 days have passed, my comrades and I have not forgotten October 7. We have not forgotten the murdered and the massacred, the raped and mutilated, the kidnapped and the missing.

Those memories were still fresh in my mind in the early afternoon, when I joined Gabrielle and a group from our community for a short visit to the site of the Nova music festival and massacre. I'm sure the experience felt raw for the hundreds of visitors we saw there, but for me the site already feels curated and sanitised, a stark difference from the forest filled with burnt-out vehicles, tents, and bodies that I remember from my first days here.

On my way back to my base, I stopped briefly at the bomb shelters at the entrance to Kibbutz Re'im, where memorial candles are lit next to gouged-out areas of concrete, twin testaments to those murdered here when terrorists tossed grenades into the crowded shelters and homes including my family.

Upon returning, I noticed a group of soldiers tending the memorial grove on the base, where each tree has a sign in memory of a fallen soldier from a unit posted here. The group was moving two rows of tall fir trees to make space for a full new row of tiny saplings.

I went to sleep in preparation for another night shift. But I was awoken by the sound of music and found my way to a sight that brought me to tears. A crowd of soldiers and civilians, religious and nonreligious, young and old, dancing their hearts out to a jumble of electronic trance music and Jewish music.

On October 6, we were a country divided, ripped apart by political disagreement, uncertain of our future as a society.

On October 7, an enemy bent on destroying us murdered more than 1,000 Israelis, including hundreds at a peaceful music festival.

On January 28, our differences haven't disappeared, and our grief is deep, and our world has changed. But amid the disagreements and the debates and the grief, we are dancing together and finding joy, and I for one am certain that our future is bright.

Thursday, February 1, 9:24 p.m.

Just as we arrived in the middle of the night more than 100 days ago, so too our unit left Gaza overnight, under cover of darkness.

I did not march in a parade, where Israelis would be throwing flowers at me and my comrades in arms. Instead, we travelled in relative silence. Perhaps it was the late hour, half of us exhausted from a long shift and the other half just awake from a partial night's sleep.

Perhaps we were weighed down by the events of our last day, during which a coordinated attack on our unit exacted a heavy price.

I am certain my unit will be ordered to re-enter the hell of Gaza in the near future. I'm not looking forward to it.

LIFE IN THE LUCKY COUNTRY

CHAPTER 8

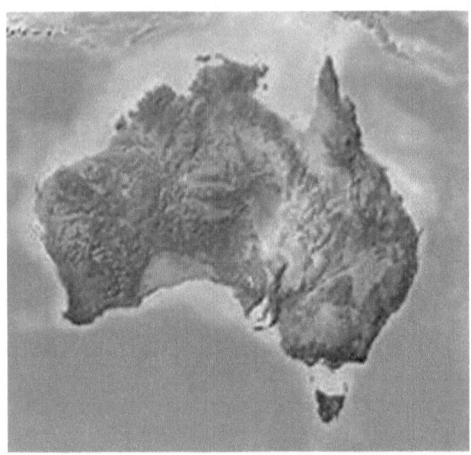

Ibrahim and Ashan had settled into a backpackers' residence as a temporary measure. Uncle Fahad had contacted the Imam and asked if he could keep an eye out for the boys.

Fahad rang them on a weekly basis to see how they were coping.

'Hello, Ibrahim how are you and Ashan enjoying your new life in Melbourne?' he asked.

'We are enjoying all that Melbourne has to offer. Yesterday we visited the National Art gallery— it was amazing.

'Walking down Bourke Street Mall is an experience! Just window shopping is exciting and we hope one day we will be able to purchase something from these wonderful stores.'

'Have you thought about how you will earn the money to do such a thing?'

'As a matter of fact, Uncle we have both decided to enrol in one of the universities. I have decided to pursue a career in Civil Engineering and Ashan wishes to pursue IT,' said Ibrahim.

'How will you pay your fees?'

'The Australian Government introduced the HECS scheme where by your fees are covered until you graduate and find employment. Once you begin to earn a salary you are required to repay the loan in monthly instalments.'

Ibrahim did not divulge the fact that he intended to approach the American Embassy in relation to the Hamas tunnels map. He had no idea how much it was worth.

After the phone call, he turned to his friend. 'Ashan, I have decided it is time I tried to sell the Hamas map.'

'How do you intend to do that?'

'There is an American Consulate right here in Melbourne. I am going to ask for an appointment with the Military Attaché.'

'Good luck with that.'

'Come on, Ashan. I'm sure they will be more than interested. If they purchase it and then pass it onto the Israelis they may be able to find the hostages.'

'When will you be approaching them and how much do you think we can get for it?' ventured Ashan.

'It's hard to tell. I think we should get them to put a price on it. I intend to go to the consulate tomorrow.'

Ibrahim caught a tram down St Kilda Road the next day. Conveniently the tram stop was opposite the American Consulate.

After Ibrahim crossed the busy road, he looked up at the imposing building and began to have second thoughts.

What if they dismissed him as a deranged Arab or searched him for weapons… which of cause they would.

'Come on Ibrahim,' he told himself. 'You have nothing to worry about. The worst that could happen is they reject my proposition and show me the door.'

The young man from Gaza approached the receptionist.

'Excuse me miss— my name is Ibrahim Salah. I am a refugee from Gaza. I escaped from Hamas's clutches with a detailed map of all their tunnels. I wish to speak with a senior embassy official.'

The receptionist answered, 'I will notify our Military Attaché. He may or may not wish to speak to you. Please take a seat in the waiting room.'

Ibrahim waited for an hour before he approached the receptionist again.

'He obviously has no intention in meeting me. I will be on my way.'

'Please don't go, Mr Salah. The attaché is a very busy man. I will call him and remind him of your presence and imminent departure.' She gave him a brief smile and spoke into a mouthpiece. 'Just a reminder, sir. Mr Salah is still waiting to see you and suggests he might as well leave. What should I tell him?'

'I haven't forgotten him, Rosy. I've been on the telephone to the ambassador. Tell him I will be with him in five minutes. Have him go up to the second floor.'

'Thank you sir. I'll let him know.'

Ibrahim did as he was asked, and another receptionist asked him to take a seat.

I hope he doesn't keep me too long. I have a lecture to attend, Ibrahim thought.

The wait was only ten minutes before a very distinguished man with silver hair came out of his office to greet him.

'Mr Salah, I'm pleased to meet you. My name is Andrew Schofields. Please come into my office.'

Ibrahim followed the man and they sat down on either side of a desk.

'Now, how can I be of assistance?'

Ibrahim recounted his amazing adventure and informed Schofields of how he had acquired the Hamas tunnels map.

'Well you have an amazing story, Ibrahim. Maybe you should write a book about your adventures.'

'Maybe one day when this horrible war is over… right now I prefer to be below the radar.'

'Yes, I get your meaning. What is it you want from me?'

'I wish to sell the Gaza tunnel network map. I am sure the USA and Israel would want it. It would facilitate rescuing the hostages and help destroy Hamas.'

'May I see the map, Ibrahim?'

Ibrahim nodded. 'Yes, although I have brought only half the map. The other half is located in a secure place.'

'Why only half?'

'As much as I trust you and the American Government we are holding onto the other half for insurance.'

'We? Who is we?'

'My friend who escaped with me.'

'What's his name?'

'With the greatest respect, I don't think you need to know that.'

'You are playing a very dangerous game my boy. What's to stop me arresting you and flying you back to Guatemala Bay in Cuba where our operatives will have a way of making you divulge the location of the other half?'

'I have no idea of its location… again this is insurance.'

'Okay, I'll contact our Embassy in Canberra they will decide whether to contact the Pentagon.'

'Thank you sir. You can contact me on 0429 444 678. It is a ghost phone so you will not be able to trace it.'

'May I keep the map to show my superiors?'

'Yes, why not.'

Ibrahim left the consulate feeling quietly confident that a deal could be struck. He returned to the backpackers and informed Ashan of the details of the meeting with Schofields.

Ibrahim had no idea how long it would be before he received an answer.

In the meantime the two began their courses at Melbourne University.

Six weeks passed before Ibrahim received a call on his mobile phone. The caller was General David Crooks in Washington.

'Hello. My name is General Crooks. My team at the Pentagon have reviewed your tunnel map… albeit only a partial document. We are keen to receive the remaining half.'

'That can certainly be arranged, General,' said Ibrahim. 'You only need to pay a reasonable amount.'

'What do you call a "reasonable amount"?'

Ibrahim took a deep breath. 'One million dollars.'

'I'm afraid your expectation is way too high young man. We were thinking of a hundred thousand.'

'If you look at how many US dollars is being spent every day during this war what we are asking seems insignificant,' argued Ibrahim. 'What price do you put on rescuing the hostages? What price do you place on the number of IDF soldiers killed in battle? What price do you put on the thousands of innocent Palestinians? I think one million is very reasonable.'

'Okay, I will speak to my superiors and get back to you.'

'Don't take too long, General. Every day delayed will be more lives lost.'

Four days later the US Government agreed to the asking price. The full amount was deposited in the joint account in the Commonwealth Bank.

Ibrahim scanned the map and sent it via email to the embassy.

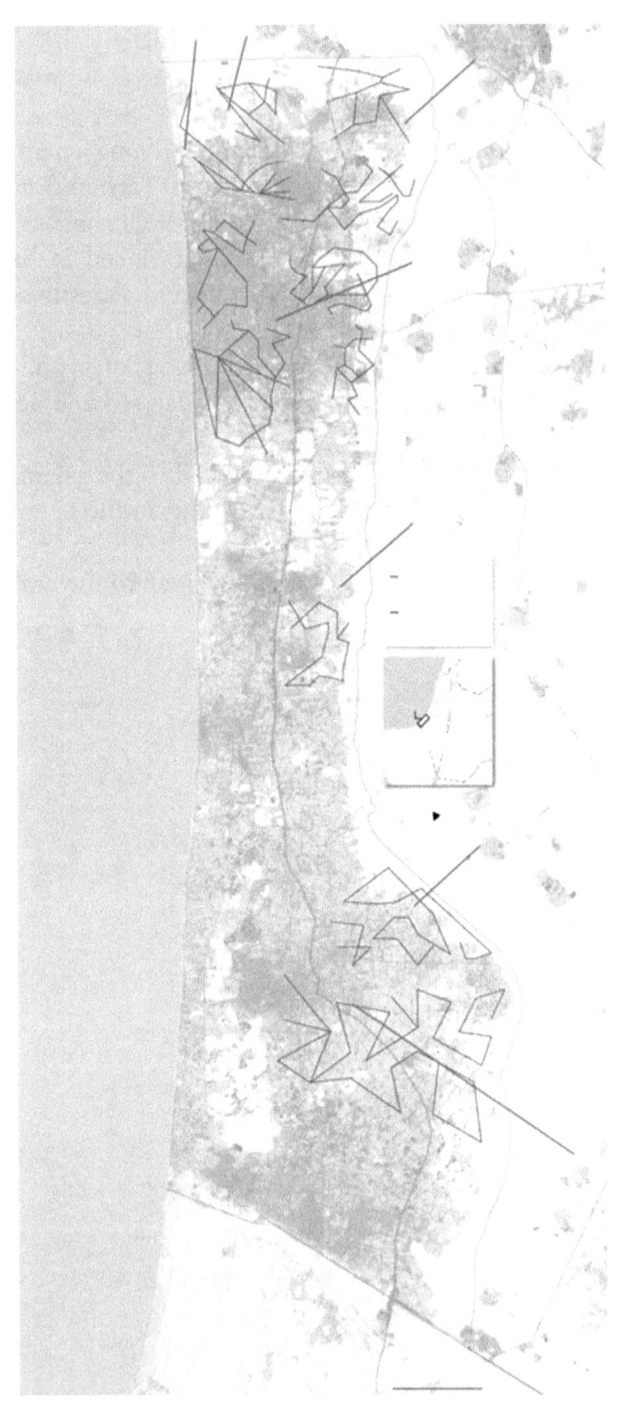

LIFE AFTER OCTOBER 7

CHAPTER 9

After Ethan's tour of duty he hoped to be admitted into the Hebrew University of Jerusalem; the second oldest University in Israel. After what he witnessed in Gaza he hoped to enlist in the Medical faculty. Being the only surviving member of his family ensured he had the resources to pay the $15,000 a year tuition fees and the $12,000 accommodation costs.

Student Quarters

Ethan's grades from year twelve ensured he was accepted into medical school. His first day was a daunting experience. He felt like a fish out of water. Ethan knew only one other student; Joseph who had begun his medical studies the year before.

'So Ethan, you are about to begin a new chapter in your life,' said Joseph.

'Yes, I suppose I am. I'm feeling a bit anxious.'

'Don't— you are a bright kid and you should fly through. I have a few suggestions in relation to what you will need in your first couple of days.

'Great. What are they?'

Joseph handed him a list.

Student ID

Diary/notebooks

Campus map, you can get an app on your phone.

Textbooks for your subjects

Stationery including pens, pencils, highlighters and folders

A laptop

And most importantly:

Lunch and snacks

Money for coffee!

Ethan thanked him.

'Would you like me to show you around the campus?' Joseph asked.

'That would be great. I feel it's all a bit overwhelming.'

'Let's start at the most important building on campus,' Joseph said, grinning.

'Would that be the medical school?'

'No, the student union building incorporating the canteen. It's where you can relax listen to cool music and play cards or chess.'

The time came for Ethan to attend his first lecture.

The lecture hall was packed with expectant medical students.

A very well-dressed woman entered the hall and stood at the lectern.

'Congratulations! You've got into medical school, and that in and of itself is a huge accomplishment. I wanted to welcome you to the medical student community and give a few pieces of advice. The next couple of years will be tough, exciting, exhausting, exhilarating... a roller coaster of emotions, I'm sure.

'Every medical school in every country is vastly different, but this blog post hopes to provide some general advice that I think can be helpful for first year medical students to hear before (or as) they embark on this tremendous journey.'

The students waited expectantly as the lecturer began to read.

'The things I learned along the way:

1. Study a little every day. If you were a last-minute kind of student in high school, you might be shocked to realise that that strategy most likely won't get you far. Be prepared to do some work at least every day so that it doesn't all accumulate right before your exams.

2. Motivation vs. discipline. It's nice to be motivated, definitely, but ultimately it comes down to discipline; doing what you need to, even when you don't want to.

3. Medical school is a marathon, so prepare for it as such. The key is long-term balance in all aspects of your life, and it's helpful to build stamina. Start studying bit by bit and build up your study day to multiple hours (as needed); add in exercise, eating right, social life, etc. until you've achieved balance. Build habits and stick to them.

4. Schedule in time off, be it nightly, weekly, monthly.

5. Prioritise. Decide what is important to you – for example prioritise proper sleep and regular exercise.

6. Be curious about every subject because they're all in your curriculum for a reason. It's much easier to study a subject when you're interested in it, so if you're inherently uninterested, at least try to approach each subject as, 'Let me learn this now, because one day I may use this to help my future patients.' It truly helps.

7. Attitude makes a huge difference. Think, 'I get to study,' not, 'I have to study.' Wake up in the morning and think, 'Today is going to be a good day,' not, 'ugh.' It makes a whole world of difference. If you find yourself shifting into a negative mindset, actively practise reframing.

8. Planning days can be really helpful; I'd use every Sunday to get an overview of my upcoming week, schedule in any classes, appointments, gym sessions and activities I had planned. This set the mood for my whole week, and I went into it knowing exactly what I had to do and where I needed to be.

9. Experiment with different study methods; I changed my study approach quite a few times in the first year as I was trying to figure out what worked best for me.

10. Ask and answer questions in class; this is important for a few reasons. For one, it helps build strong relationships with your professors, because it shows that you are listening and that you're curious. Secondly, it requires paying attention, and it really helps

reinforce your learning; also, when you're trying to understand a topic on your own later, you'll wish you had asked the question.

11. Notes in class. I always recommend taking notes in class, because I think this converts the typical passive listening class attendance into a much more engaging, interactive active participation class. This, once again, reinforces your learning. Also, things often make the most sense during class, so if you jot it down, it'll be easier to jog your memory.

12. Help one another. This should go without saying, but sadly it isn't always the case. If you're struggling, ask for help; if you missed a class, ask for notes. There is no shame in it, and when someone asks the same from you, don't hesitate to help them out. You're all in it together – you're not competing against each other, although sometimes it might feel like it. Believe me, you'll come out much stronger together; socialise, make friends, and definitely surround yourself with people that you can rely on, and who can count on you.

13. Study to save lives. The age-old saying might seem corny, but it truly is a humbling, motivating feeling thinking that the knowledge you gain today might help you down the line. Medical school builds on itself – anatomy might not seem crucial, but surgery, neurology, etc. build heavily on it, so study the theory now so that you can be a great clinician/surgeon one day.

14. Medical school is a process. I alluded to this in the previous point, but I think it's really important to mention again because you might not realise how medical school gradually builds upon itself. In first year, you will be inundated with a landslide of information and feel you're drowning, but you'll survive, believe me. And you may not notice it because the change is so gradual, but your knowledge will build on itself slowly and surely. Before you know it, you'll be throwing medical jargon around like Dr House and his team, unaware of how far you've come.

15. Don't allow yourself to get caught up in grades. Sometimes, lots of studying might still land you with a poor grade, and it can be heart wrenching. I've fallen into the trap myself, but the gist of it is this: the knowledge that you gained while studying for your exam can never be taken from you. If you studied hard, learned the material, and had a bad day or bad examiner or stomach bug and got a bad grade – it doesn't matter as much as the fact that you know your stuff.'

She looked up and smiled.

'Medical school isn't the be all and end all of your life; I highly recommend doing things outside medical school. I think medical school is largely about balance. Work until you're satisfied with the way your life is divided – this can be incredibly challenging, especially at first. It took me quite a while to achieve the kind of balance in my life that I'm more or less satisfied with, and I've had to learn some of these lessons the hard way.

'It's going to be amazing. You've worked really hard to be right where you are, and you should be proud. Medical school is an incredible journey, and I hope you love it as much as I did.'

YEMEN HOME OF THE HOUTHI

CHAPTER 10

Fighting between Houthi rebels and the Saudi coalition that backs Yemen's internationally recognised government has largely subsided, but Houthis have repeatedly attacked ships transiting the Red Sea in response to Israel's war on Hamas. Dialogue between the Houthis and Saudi Arabia, along with Iranian-Saudi normalisation, has provided hope for a negotiated solution. However, talks have yielded little progress and have been punctuated by violence. The Southern Transitional Council (STC) has also renewed calls for an independent southern Yemeni state, complicating peace prospects, and al-Qaeda in the Arabian Peninsula (AQAP) attacks have surged.

al-Qaeda Leader

Meanwhile, the humanitarian crisis has not improved; 21.6 million people need aid, including 11 million children, and more than 4.5 million are displaced.

Background

Yemen's civil war began in 2014 when Houthi insurgents—Shiite rebels with links to Iran and a history of rising up against the Sunni government control of Yemen's capital and largest city, Sanaa, demanding lower fuel prices and a new government. Following failed negotiations, the rebels seized the presidential palace in January 2015, leading President Abd Rabbu Mansour Hadi and his government to resign.

In March 2015, a coalition of Gulf States led by Saudi Arabia launched a campaign of economic sanctions and air strikes against the Houthi insurgents, with the support of the US.

In February 2015, after escaping from Sanaa, Hadi rescinded his resignation, but a Houthi advance forced Hadi to flee Aden for exile in Saudi Arabia. While he attempted to return to Aden he ultimately ruled as president in exile.

The intervention of regional powers in Yemen's conflict also drew the country into a regional struggle incorporating the Sunni-Shia divide. In June 2015, Saudi Arabia implemented a naval blockade to prevent Iran from supplying the Houthis with sophisticated weapons. Iran responded by dispatching a naval convoy, raising the risk of military escalation between the two countries. The militarisation of Yemen's waters also included the US Navy, which continued to seize Yemen-bound Iranian weapons. The blockade has been the catalyst for the humanitarian crisis throughout the conflict. Saudi Arabia and the United Arab Emirates have exercised a massive campaign, carrying out over twenty-five thousand air strikes. These strikes have caused over nineteen thousand civilian casualties, and from 2021 to 2022 the Houthis responded with a spate of drone attacks on Saudi Arabia and the UAE.

Houthis Attack Saudi Arabia

Saudi Bombing Raid

The Houthis embarked on a blitzkrieg, making fast progress at the start of the war, moving eastward to Marib and then pushing south to Aden in early 2015. A counter attack by the Saudis pushed the Houthis back north and west until a stable front line was established. A UN effort to broker peace talks between allied Houthi rebels and the internationally recognised Yemeni government stalled in the summer of 2016. A menacing force had been established al-Qaeda threatened Government control in the south.

In July 2016, the Houthis and the government of former President Saleh, ousted in 2011 after nearly thirty years in power, announced the formation of a political council to govern Sana'a and much of northern Yemen. However, in December 2017, Saleh broke with the Houthis and called for his followers to take up arms against them. Saleh was killed and his forces were defeated within two days.

President Saleh

Houthis Rebels

Meanwhile, Hadi and his allies faced their own challenge: the Sothern Transitional Council. Established in 2017, the STC grew out of the southern separatist movement that predates the civil war and controls areas in the southwest around and including Aden. A 2019 Saudi brokered incorporated the STC into the internationally recognised governments, but the faction could still be a danger.

In 2018, coalition forces made an offensive push on the coast northward to the strategic city of Hodeidah, the main seaport for northern Yemen. The fighting ended in a ceasefire the ceasefire largely held but fighting continued elsewhere. Taiz, Yemen's third largest city also remained a hot point having been blockaded by the Houthis since 2015. In 2020, the UAE officially withdrew from Yemen, but still maintains extensive influence in the country.

In February 2021, Houthi rebels launched an offensive to seize the ancient city of Marib.

In early March, and Houthi rebels conducted missile air strikes in Saudi Arabia, including targeting oil tankers and facilities and international airports.

The Saudi-led coalition responded to the air attacks with air strikes targeting Sanaa. The offensive was the deadliest clash since 2018, killing hundreds of fighters and complicating the peace processes.

Meanwhile, the conflict has taken a heavy toll on Yemeni civilians, making Yemen the world's worst humanitarian crisis. The UN estimated that 60 percent of the estimated 377,000 deaths in Yemen between 2015 and the beginning of 2022 were the result of indirect causes like food insecurity and lack of accessible health services. Two-thirds of the population, or 21.6 million Yemenis, remain in dire need of assistance. Five million are at risk of famine, and a cholera outbreak has affected over one million people. All sides of the conflict are reported to have violated human rights and international humanitarian law.

An economic crisis continues to compound the ongoing humanitarian crisis. In late 2019, the conflict led to the splintering of the economy into two broad economic zones under territories controlled by the Houthis and the Saudi-backed government. In the fall of 2021, the sharp depreciation of Yemen's currency, particularly in government-controlled areas, significantly reduced people's purchasing power and pushed many basic necessities even further out of reach, leading to widespread protests across cities in southern Yemen.

Security forces forcefully responded to the protests.

Separate from the ongoing civil war, the United States is suspected of conducting counterterrorism operations in Yemen, relying mainly on air strikes to target al-Qaeda in the Arabian Peninsula (AQAP) and militants associated with the self-proclaimed Islamic State. The United States is deeply invested in combating terrorism and violent extremism in Yemen, having collaborated with the Yemeni government on counterterrorism since the bombing of the USS Cole in 2000. Since 2002, the United States has carried out nearly four hundred strikes in Yemen.

In April 2016, the United States deployed a small team of forces to advise and assist Saudi-led troops to retake territory from AQAP. In January 2017, a US Special Operations Force in central Yemen killed one US service member; several suspected AQAP-affiliated fighters, and an unknown number of Yemeni civilians. Breaking from previous US policy, President Joe Biden the then President announced an end of US support for Saudi-led offensive operations in Yemen in February 2021 and revoked its designation of the Houthis as a terrorist organisation. In January 2024, the Houthis were redesignated as a terrorist organisation due to their recent attacks on ships in the Red Sea and Gulf of Aden.

Houthis have sunk many foreign ships

In April 2022, Yemen's internationally recognised but unpopular president, Abd Rabbu Mansour Hadi, resigned after ten years in power to make way for a new seven-member presidential council. Rashad al-Alimi, Hadi adviser with close ties to Saudi Arabia and powerful Yemeni politicians, chairs the new council.

Peace talks between Saudi and Houthi officials, mediated by Oman, resumed in April 2023, but little has been achieved. The discussions were reportedly centred on a complete reopening of Houthi-controlled ports and Sanaa airport, reconstruction efforts, and a timeline for foreign forces to withdraw from Yemen. Negotiations have also been overshadowed by the suspension of the only commercial air route out of Sanaa and a Houthi drone attack that killed four Bahraini members of the Saudi-led coalition didn't improve things.

Talks held between Iran and Saudi Arabia in April 2023, mediated by China, raised hopes of a political settlement to end the conflict in Yemen. The talks led to a breakthrough agreement to re-establish diplomatic relations and re-open both sides' embassies after years of tension and hostility.

While hostility between the two warring sides remains low, AQAP's political violence surged. Most of the violence has been centred on Yemen's Abyan and Shawba factions. AQAP has used drones and IEDs to target forces affiliated with the STC. In August 2023, AQAP launched an explosion that killed a military commander and three soldiers from the Security Belt Forces, an armed group loyal to the STC. Earlier that month, AQAP fighters killed five troops from another force affiliated with the separatist council. The recent use of drones by AQAP in Yemen's south is likely an attempt to reassert its influence in the area despite its waning influence, and some believe that this sudden and sustained use of drones signals external support. Additionally, AQAP has continued its anti-separatist efforts, with further attacks targeting and wounding five STC-backed fighters.

Three days after the October 7 attack on Israel, Yemen's Houthi leader Abdel-Malek al-Houthi warned that if the United States intervenes in the Hamas-Israel War directly, the group will respond by taking military action. In mid-October, US officials announced that the USS Carney downed several Houthi cruise missiles and drones fired towards Israel.

USS Carney

The Houthis continued to launch several rounds of missiles and drones until it officially proclaimed its entry into the war to support Palestinians in the Gaza Strip on October 31. Houthi attacks of the same nature continued into November. On November 19, the Houthis hijacked a commercial ship in the Red Sea and have since attacked many more with drones, missiles, and speedboats as of late January 2024.

Houthis Pirates

As a result, major shipping companies have ceased using the Red Sea—through which almost 15 percent of global seaborne trade passes—and have rerouted to take longer and costlier journeys around Southern Africa instead. The situation has resulted in heightened shipping and insurance costs. In response to the consistent Houthi attacks in the Red Sea, the United States and United Kingdom carried out coordinated air strikes on Houthi targets in Yemen on January 11 and January 22. It is unclear whether the attacks will cease in the near future, with the Houthis promising to persist in their military operations until a ceasefire is agreed to in the Gaza Strip and aid is allowed into the enclave.

HOME IS WHERE THE HEART IS

CHAPTER 11

Death and Destruction

Following the Israel-Hamas ceasefire, the Saleh family made their long journey to Gaza's north after 15 months of displacement. There, they found their home destroyed.

Klialed and his family were among the over half a million Palestinians who made the long journey north along the Netzarim corridor, which Israel recently reopened as part of a ceasefire deal with Hamas.

Netzarim Corridor

Like many others, Klialed made the journey on foot, together with his wife Hannan and their two remaining children Ahmed and Mona.. They walked over five hours from Deir Al-Balah in central Gaza, some 20 kilometres away.

Deir Al-Balah

'We left at around seven in the morning. The road ahead of us was extremely difficult. There was no water or food on the route,' said Klialed.

When the family returned to the home that took Klialed almost his whole life to obtain, they found it destroyed.

'I left it for approximately one-and-a-half years and returned to find it in ruins. It was very difficult, a horrible feeling.'

More than a year of displacement

For 15 months, Klialed's family had been living in makeshift tents, displaced four times. The first time came just days after Hamas' 7th of October attack on Israel.

'On the first day, on 7 October, we were woken up at six in the morning by the sound of missile strikes, a huge amount. We did not know what was happening,' Klialed explained.

'We waited until nine in the morning until we then discovered there had been a huge offensive. Hamas had invaded Israeli territory. Israel then launched a full-scale war on the Gaza Strip.' The horror had begun.

Amid intense Israeli bombardment, Klialed and his family first fled to Deir Al-Balah, then Khan Younis, and eventually Rafah, before ending up back in Deir Al-Balah, where they remained for almost a year.

Life in tents provided little protection from the cold and rain. Klialed explained that returning home meant they would at least have a roof over their heads. But now, they fear it may collapse on them at any moment.

'The house that I am in is half here, half gone. At any given moment, God forbid, it could collapse,' he said. 'We are living on a miracle and risking everything, risking myself, my family, and my sister's children, just to shelter ourselves from the hardships of winter.'

Even though staying in a tent would be safer, Klialed says he has no other option.

'When I am in a tent, my life is guaranteed; there is no risk of a roof suddenly collapsing on top of me,' he says, adding that 'if I could find another house to stay in, I would, but it's not possible.'

Rebuilding Gaza could take 350 years, UN says

Israeli bombardment and ground operations have transformed entire neighbourhoods into wastelands. The north, Klialed's home, is the most heavily destroyed part of Gaza.

This has made it incredibly difficult for much-needed humanitarian aid to reach the population there, even since the start of the ceasefire.

The United Nations said humanitarian organisations are expanding their operational presence and services in areas that were previously hard or impossible to access, including the north.

Over the past weeks, the World Food Programme (WFP) delivered more than 10 million metric tonnes of food to the Strip, reaching roughly 1 million people through food parcel distributions to households.

But for Klialed, basic needs like food, water and health care have become more difficult to access since the ceasefire. He says that while he had to travel far to receive aid while displaced, it now takes him even longer to obtain water or reach the nearest hospital.

'It is very, very difficult,' he said. 'My house is about a half-hour away from where we can get water. I have to carry all the bottles with me, and then walk back for another half-hour. It became more difficult than before, to a large degree.'

Although humanitarian organisations have increased their presence in the north, the complete absence of infrastructure means some areas remain impossible to reach, leaving thousands of people like Klialed without access to essential items.

The UN said that out of 25 emergency medical teams in the Gaza Strip, only one operates in the north. It added that while 565,092 people travelled north amid the ceasefire, more than 45,678 have been heading southwards due to the lack of services and the widespread destruction of homes and communities.

Using satellite data, the UN estimated last month that 69% of the structures in Gaza have been damaged or destroyed, including over 245,000 homes. The World Bank estimated $18.5 billion in damage — nearly the combined economic output of the West Bank and Gaza in 2022 — from just the first four months of the war.

It says that it could take more than 350 years to rebuild if the Israeli blockade, imposed in 2007 when Hamas took power, remains.

And it's unclear when — or even if — much will be rebuilt. That's mainly come into question as US President Donald Trump suggested that displaced Palestinians in Gaza be permanently resettled outside the war-torn territory, while the US should take "ownership" of the enclave.

Human rights organisations such as Human Rights Watch have warned that such a plan would amount to ethnic cleansing.

Even if Palestinians are not expelled from Gaza en masse, many fear that they will never be able to return to their homes or that the destruction wreaked on the territory will make it impossible to live there.

After Trump's statement, US officials, including Secretary of State Marco Rubio, have said he only sought to move the roughly 1.8 million Gazan citizens temporarily to allow for reconstruction.

But many Palestinians, including Klialed, have already said they will not leave their homes. 'From our side, as Palestinians, this premise is completely rejected,' he said.

'We spent a year-and-a-half under war; we will not accept the idea of leaving,' Klialed added. 'Those who leave their own countries suffer unspeakably. We will not leave or flee our country.'

Klialed

YOUNG MEDICS IN LOVE

CHAPTER 12

Ethan felt quite nervous walking into the cavernous lecture hall, and he made his way to the back row so as not to bring attention to himself.

A very beautiful young woman took her seat beside him. Both nodded but did not speak.

It appeared that each subsequent lecture they were seated next to each other, each time nodding but not speaking.

Finally Ethan got the courage to say something.

'We seem to be destined to sit next to each other.'

'So it would seem.'

'My name is Ethan.'

'Pleased to finally meet you Ethan. My name is Hannah.'

That was the extent of their communication; it took another two weeks of polite conversation before Ethan built up the courage to ask Hannah to join him for a coffee in the student lounge.

The two students sat down at a table in the small coffee lounge and ordered their coffees, a cappuccino for Hannah while Ethan ordered a long black.

'So what's the Hannah story?' Ethan asked.

'What do you mean?'

'Where were you born?'

'Here, in Jerusalem.'

'Were your parents also born here?'

'No. My father was born in Hungary and my mother was born in Poland. They immigrated here after the war and met through becoming worshipers at Karaite Synagogue.'

'Are they still alive?'

'No.'

'I'm sorry.'

'Don't be. They both lived to a good age. They both survived the Holocaust but their parents and siblings did not.'

'Excuse me for asking these questions. I've been accused of interviewing people. I'm just interested in life stories.'

'I have no problem in answering them.'

'Okay, one more. Do you have any siblings?'

'I have a brother who is a doctor. My sister was kidnapped on October 7. I have no idea if she is still alive.'

'How sad.'

'And now it's my turn, Ethan. Tell me about your family.'

'My mother and father and sister were murdered by Hamas in their home at the Be'eri kibbutz.'

'Oh my God, so I assume you are the sole survivor.'

'I am.'

'I'm sorry.'

'Don't be. They were only three of 1200 slaughtered that terrible day.'

'I had no problem invading Gaza when I was a soldier in the IDF.'

'Yes, Hamas must pay but I have great sympathy for the thousands of innocents that have lost their lives.'

'So do I. Collateral damage is inevitable in war, unfortunately.'

Ethan and Hannah continued to sit next to each other in most of their lectures and continued to have coffee together and sometimes lunch. It was obvious to both of them that the relationship was evolving into something special.

Ethan suggested he and Hannah attend the Radiohead concert, which was held in support of Israel. She agreed they decided to have dinner at Hannah's favourite restaurant before the concert.

They made their way to the restaurant, which was close to the concert venue. 'Piccolino' happened to be a favourite eating house for the both of them.

Hannah ordered spinach cannelloni while Ethan ordered calamari fritti and they shared a bottle white wine.

Afterwards, they attended the concert.

Paranoid Android, Creep, Fake Plastic Trees and Everything in Its Right Place were their favourite numbers, although they both enjoyed the entire concert. Everybody in the large audience appreciated the group playing in support of Israel.

'Well that was a great concert. It's amazing that one of the best groups in the world would come to Israel in the middle of a war,' said Hannah afterwards.

'I agree. When you see the demonstrations supporting the Palestinians all over the world it makes you wonder.'

'I'd like to see their reactions if they were caught up in the slaughter on October 7th.'

'Don't get me wrong— I'm horrified by the number of casualties in Gaza, but we need to eliminate Hamas,' said Hannah.

War is horrible especially for the innocents; 31 million civilians were killed in WW1 and WW2,' said Ethan. He grimaced. 'Let's change the subject. If you had your choice where would you travel to in the summer break?'

'That's easy. Paris.'

'That's good because I've booked two flights to Paris departing in five days.'

'You're kidding.'

'No, I'm not. Pack your bag, babe.'

'I don't believe it. Where will we stay?'

'Here. I have brought a photo of Hotel Turenne Marais. It is located in the 4th arrondissement which is close to everything you would wish to visit in Paris.'

The time couldn't go quickly enough for Hannah. She had always dreamed of a visit to the city of lights.

Finally the day came for the four-and-a-half-hour flight. Ethan had booked business class. He was going to make sure it would be a wonderful experience for Hannah. His secret plan was to ask Hannah to marry him under the Eiffel Tower. The ring he purchased was a one-caret diamond.

On arrival at Charles de Gaulle Airport they were selected by customs for a luggage and body search. The customs officer, who was a Palestinian immigrant, cleared them.

They caught a taxi to their hotel, checked in and went up to their room on the sixth floor.

That night they dined at Chez Janou, a fantastic little restaurant offering a taste of Provençale cuisine in Paris.

They enjoyed their meal and returned to the hotel where they made love for the first time.

The next morning Ethan decided to go down to the street and buy a newspaper. Unknown to him the custom officer had alerted a terrorist cell of the Israeli tourists' arrival and the hotel where they were staying.

They couldn't believe their luck. Standing in front of their car was their target. Five bullets from an AK47 hit Ethan in the chest and head, and he died instantly.

Hannah heard the police sirens and the siren of an ambulance and when Ethan hadn't returned after a half an hour she went down to see if she could find him. She arrived just as Ethan's body was being loaded into the ambulance.

No! She tried to see him in the ambulance, but the gendarme prevented her. She fell to her knees crying uncontrollably.

'What happened— did he get hit by a car?'

'Madam I take it you know the victim and I can understand your grief but unfortunately I cannot divulge how he died until a post-mortem is conducted,' said the senior gendarme.

A week passed before Hannah was called into the coroner's office. She was informed of the shooting. She was also informed that Ethan died instantly and would not have felt any pain. That was some consolation for losing his life so young. She requested that his body be flown back to Israel for a Jewish burial. Her request was granted.

Hannah flew back on El Al; it was an uncomfortable flight knowing the only man she ever loved was in the cargo hold.

The funeral was a small affair and there was no family in attendance as they had been murdered by Hamas just as Ethan had been. Apart from Hannah, a small number of medical students attended.

Hannah was not aware that prior to the Paris trip Ethan had intended to propose. He already made Hannah his sole beneficiary in his will. His estate amounted to $2.000,000 and she would be wealthy for the rest of her life.

Hannah went on to finish her medical degree and she committed herself to help the underprivileged both in Israel and Gaza.

She purchased an apartment in Jerusalem for 2,200,000 shekels, which equated to US$840,000.

YOU GO YOUR WAY I'LL GO MINE

CHAPTER 13

March One 2025

The first day at Melbourne University was daunting for the two Palestinian teenagers. The first task was to go to the bookshop and purchase the books required by their respective book lists.

They both enjoyed Orientation week but now the real work would begin.

Ibrahim's ambition once he became a qualified civil engineer was to return to Gaza and help rebuild the place he loved. The estimates calculated by the UN were $400 billion to rebuild and that the work would not be complete until 2045. A long road lay ahead for the people of Gaza.

Ashan had no ambition to return to Gaza. He hoped to start his own software company when he qualified and generate wealth.

Ashan was approached by a follow Palestinian who was also studying I.T.

'I believe you escaped from the mayhem of Gaza. No doubt you left your homeland when you witnessed the death and destruction the Jews inflicted on us.'

'Yes. I knew I had no future there.'

'What's your name?' the man asked.

'Ashan.'

'And I am Iman.' He smiled briefly. 'Well Ashan, I would like to invite you to our discussion group. We are ten Palestinians who have immigrated to Australia to find a better life.'

'I would be interested…but I'll hear what you all have to say before I make my decision.'

'Our next meeting is next Saturday at the townhouse of one of our members, Mohamed. What's your address? I will pick you up.'

Ashan gave his address and asked, 'What time?

'Around 8 pm.'

Ashan nodded. 'I'll look forward to meeting fellow Palestinians from Gaza.'

Iman was right on time and they drove to Mohamed's townhouse in Carlton.

The other members had already arrived and were drinking coffee.

Once Iman and Ashan had settled in the discussion began. Mohamed began by welcoming everybody and then introduced the topic for discussion. It was no surprise that the evening's topic was the future of Gaza.

A common thread of discussion was their hate for the Jews and how they should retaliate.

They also discussed how they could make a contribution to the rebuilding of their homeland.

Ashan sat and listened and by the end of the evening he had decided to join the group.

The young man attended several meetings and soon became a convert to committing revenge on the Jewish community of Melbourne.

A suggestion was made that a powerful car bomb be parked outside one of the largest synagogues in Melbourne, the Melbourne Hebrew Congregation, with over 700 members.

'Are you sure you want to do that? If we are caught we will spend the rest of our lives in prison,' said Abeer, one of the older members of the group.

'Well, painting antisemitic slogans on the walls is not going to achieve anything. If we are careful and plan the attack carefully we should get away with it,' said Iman.

'Okay, let's have a show of hands. Hold up your hand if you support the attack.'

All but Abeer supported the motion.

'Then it's decided; we go ahead,' said Mohamed.

Over the coming months the terrorists formulated their deadly plan.

Tasks were allocated to each member. Purchasing a vehicle with cash were Ramy and his girlfriend Hana. The explosives were purchased from an outlaw bikie gang and the timer and wiring came from Bunnings. Jamal was selected to manufacture the bomb as he was a third-year electrician.

All was in place ready for the deadly task. Yom Kippur on October 2 was chosen as the date for the operation.

Abeer was concerned. Despite the fact he resented the Israeli retaliation for October 7, he could not bring himself to slaughter innocent Australian citizens.

He spent many sleepless nights thinking about what he could do to prevent the carnage. There was only one way; go to the police.

He entered the Carlton Police Station and asked to speak with the officer in charge. A tall grey haired police officer approached him at the counter.

'How can I help you, sir?'

'I have information that will save many lives from a bomb attack.'

'You'd better come to my office.'

Abeer followed the policeman into his office and was asked to sit.

'My name is Sergeant Saunders,' said the officer. 'May I ask yours?'

'Abeer. I won't give you the rest of it.'

The officer nodded his understanding. 'So Abeer, what information do you have?'

Abeer recounted the plan in detail.

'Can you give me the names of those involved in this plot?'

Abeer produced a foolscap paper with all the names of the conspirators and their addresses.

'How do you know all this?'

'Because I am a member of the group. I tried to talk them out of it, but they wouldn't listen.'

'Are they all friends of yours?'

Abeer hesitated. 'Not really.'

'You have reported a very serious crime and we will act on the information. I can assure you we will protect your identity.'

'Thank you, sir.'

Abeer left the police station with mixed feelings. On the one hand he felt vindicated but on the other he felt like a traitor.

Sergeant Saunders contacted the Federal Police and requested an immediate meeting.

It was arranged for 10 am the following day. Saunders gave a brief outline of the situation on the telephone and therefore senior Federal police officers were present in the meeting.

Once they were briefed, a decision was made to conduct raids immediately.

At five the following morning, raids were conducted on all the suspects' homes. All members of the group were arrested and transported to police headquarters.

They were charged with terrorism and incarcerated without bail. The court hearing was set for the following month, September 23rd.

The rabbi from the Melbourne Hebrew Congregation was notified and assured there was no longer a threat to his people.

The court case was held on January 24 the following year.

The defendants' lawyers could not refute the evidence, and all were sentenced to life imprisonment.

Ibrahim was devastated. He knew Ashan only as a good man who was a good student and a proud Palestinian.

The only good thing to come from this disaster was the fact that Ibrahim had control of the money that had been paid for the Gaza tunnel maps. Ashan would have no use for his share and after all it was Ibrahim who had stolen the maps and negotiated with the Americans.

Abeer knew that he had done the right thing, though how many lives he had saved he did not know.

He concentrated on his studies and was either top or near the top in all his subjects. He was popular with most of the other students, particularly the girls, who viewed him as a young Amir El Masry.

Being a Muslim meant he did not drink alcohol but that did not stop him from attending the student parties.

Ibrahim did not want to bring attention to himself, so he brought along non-alcoholic wine, and no one was the wiser.

Although Ibrahim revelled in his degree he did have an element of sadness knowing his good friend was languishing in jail.

Ibrahim began a relationship with a student called Kate. It became serious and talk of marriage began. The only obstacle was that Kate was Catholic and she refused to convert to Islam. Ibrahim could not even contemplate converting to Catholicism so sadly, the relationship ended.

Ibrahim was close to graduating.

Although he had significant funds, particularly having appointed a very good financial adviser, he was quite frugal.

By the time he graduated his net worth was $1,400,000.

He joined a very reputable Civil Engineering firm, 3W Consulting Engineering in Melbourne.

The Hamas Israeli war had finally come to a close and it was now time to rebuild the Strip.

All parties including the EU rejected talk by President Trump of turning Gaza into the Riviera of the Mediterranean.

Ibrahim was highly regarded by 3W but he felt it was his duty to return to the Middle East and help rebuild the country.

He was well aware that he would have to live in Jerusalem and cross over when required. The Israeli Government issued him with the required visa knowing a rebuilt Gaza without Hamas was essential to the region's peace. They needed all the help they could muster including builders, tradespeople, architects and civil engineers and more.

The $400 billion would come from many countries around the globe. This estimate could blow out over the next twenty years it would take for the rebuilding.

The knowledge that cities such as Berlin, Prague, Dresden, Tokyo and Hiroshima were reduced to rubble and rebuilt to become great cities again gave the citizens great hope.

Ibrahim arrived at Ben Gurian airport after a nineteen-hour flight. He had been billeted in a United Nations accommodation facility in Jerusalem together with engineers and architects from various countries.

The first briefing Ibrahim attended discussed how the rubble from Gaza's destruction would be cleared and stored.

A senior construction engineer from Britain gave a presentation.

He proposed the construction of an artificial island.

The island, proposed at some 534 hectares (1,320 acres) and at a cost of approximately $5 billion over several years, would include infrastructure to provide Gaza with essential services it currently lacked, including desalination facilities for clean water and an electricity plant, a freight harbour and an area for container storage, which Katz said would help open the Gaza economy to the outside world. A bridge would connect it to the Gaza mainland, with one portion acting as a drawbridge.

Ibrahim was impressed with the plan and looked forwards to contributing to the construction of the islands. He met another civil engineer who had a wealth of experience. Her name was Vida Erzman and she was a survivor of the Holocaust. Vida took the young engineer under her wing and he learnt many things he had not been taught at university.

18thAugust 2025

On Monday evening, a Hamas source told the BBC that the group had submitted a written response to mediators saying it agreed to the ceasefire proposal without any amendments or conditions.

According to a Palestinian official familiar with the talks, the proposal mirrors the one presented by Steve Witkoff two months ago, which Hamas rejected.

Witkoff proposed a 60-day truce that would see the release of 10 living hostages by Hamas and the bodies of 18 other hostages in exchange for Palestinian prisoners held in Israeli jails. He also said that serious negotiations to end the war would take place during the truce.

On Sunday night, hundreds of thousands of Israelis gathered in Tel Aviv to demand that their government agree a deal with Hamas to end the war now and bring all the hostages home.

Hostages' families fear that another offensive in Gaza City could endanger those held there.

'I'm scared that my son would be hurt,' said Dani Miran, whose 48-year-old son Omri has been held captive for 682 days.

Netanyahu accused the demonstrators of hardening Hamas's negotiating position.

Palestinians also called for an immediate end to the war at a protest in Gaza City on Monday.

'Hamas and its demands, and the demands being negotiated, do not represent me. I want to live in peace. I want peace of mind. Our only demand is peace and safety for our children,' one woman told a local freelance journalist working for the BBC.

US President Donald Trump meanwhile wrote on social media: 'We will only see the return of the remaining hostages when Hamas is confronted and destroyed! The sooner this takes place, the better the chances of success will be.'

Looks likely this war will continue for some time.

PUTIN'S NUT CRACKER SUITE

CHAPTER 14

UKRAINE

Area: 233,030 sq mi (603,549 sq km). Population: (2025 est.) 42,721,000. Capital: Kiev Ukrainians make up more than three-fourths of the population of Ukraine; there is a significant minority of Russians. Languages: Ukrainian Russian, Romanian, Polish, Hungarian, Belarusian, Bulgarian. Religions: Christianity (mostly Eastern Orthodox; also other Christians, Roman Catholic, Protestant), Islam.

Ukraine consists of level plains and the Carpathian Mountains, which extend through the western region for more than 240 km.

The Dnieper Southern Buh Donets, and Dniester are the major rivers. The Donets Basin in the east-central region is one of the major heavy-industrial and mining-metallurgical complexes of Europe. There, iron ore and coal are mined, and natural gas, petroleum, iron, and steel are produced. Ukraine is a major producer of winter wheat and sugar beets.

Ukraine is a unitary multiparty republic with one legislative body; its head of state is the president, and the head of government is the prime minister.

MELBOURNE AUSTRALIA

Ivan

Ivan immigrated to Australia with his family; his mother Sofia; father Mykhailo and his two sisters Maria and Marusha in 2002 seeking a better life.

Mykhailo Shevchenko had established a computer software company in Kiev in 1995 developing agricultural software to aid farmers increase their crops and improve the management of their farms. In 2000 he brought in a partner, Dymytro, a financial consultant, to become the general manager of the company, enabling Mykhailo to concentrate on managing the software development team, which had grown to fifteen software analysts and programmers.

The company "Agrisoft" was thriving. The Shevchenkos were enjoying a very comfortable lifestyle until Mykhailo discovered his partner had embezzled all the company's funds and disappeared.

This forced Agrisoft to declare bankruptcy and let all its employees go.

The Shevchenko family was now destitute. Mykhailo approached his brother to lend him money so they could immigrate to Australia and start again. Artem agreed and the family boarded a plane to Melbourne where they would begin a new life.

With the money Mykhailo's brother lent him, the family moved into a two-bedroom flat in Moorabbin, an outer Melbourne suburb.

Mykhailo was able to secure a position with a software company called Data 6 and the children were enrolled in the local state schools.

Initially, Ivan found school difficult. His English was rudimentary and as a consequence he was bullied by some of the other boys. He soon learnt to speak fluent English and how to defend himself. His grades were exceptional, and he discovered Aussie Rules football. After two years of playing he was made captain of the school team.

The other students developed a high respect for the Ukrainian immigrant, and he now enjoyed school life.

At the end of year twelve Ivan was able to enrol at Monash University to study architecture. He was the only one in his year twelve class to progress to tertiary education.

Monash University

Ivan enjoyed university life including playing in the football team and joining the chess club.

It was in his final year that he met and started dating Anna, a medical student. Anna was a fifth generation Australian with flame red hair owing to her Scottish ancestors.

Anna was about to complete her fourth year and she had only one more year to go before she started her internship at Prince Henry Hospital.

Ivan suggested they might have dinner at their favourite restaurant, The Jolly Frog in Carlton.

'What's the occasion, darling?' Anna asked.

'Nothing special. I just thought it would be nice.'

Anna laughed. 'You are an insatiable romantic, my darling.'

The couple entered the restaurant and were soon seated at their usual table.

Anton the restaurateur approached them with the menu.

'It's nice to see you back. Are you celebrating anything special?'

'No, not as far as I know,' answered Anna.

Anton left them to decide on their order.

'Anna, I have a confession to make,' Ivan said.

'You're breaking up with me!'

'Don't be silly! Of course not— I love you.'

'Then what is you want to confess?' asked Anna, puzzled.

'As you know my family immigrated from Ukraine many years ago. I have grown up in Australia and love this country very much but…'

'But what?'

'I feel obligated to defend my old country from the invading Russians.'

'I can't believe it, Ivan! You are going to put yourself in harm's way fighting these aggressors with a strong chance you will never return to me and your family?'

'I'm sorry, Anna, but I feel it is my moral duty.'

Anna stared at him. 'Well,' she said at length, 'you'd better not get shot. I need you back with me.'

Ivan and Anna did not mention the subject again throughout the meal. It was only when Ivan dropped off the love of his life that Anna asked when Ivan would be leaving.

'Next Saturday.'

'My God! That doesn't give us much time together! You'd better come inside.'

They made love with a passion neither of them felt before.

The following Saturday Anna drove her lover to Melbourne airport to board an Air France flight to Kiev— a 44-hour flight with a stop-over in Dubai. It was a heartfelt goodbye to Anna; Ivan had mixed feelings but he knew he was doing the right thing. Anna cried most of the way home.

Ivan was exhausted by the time he entered Kiev Airport; he had contacted the recruitment centre from Melbourne, so he knew where to direct the taxi. Despite his exhaustion he went straight to the army recruitment centre.

He entered what looked like any other office building. There was a receptionist sitting at the front desk— the only difference was she was dressed in an army uniform.

When Ivan introduced himself, she checked his name on the computer and then asked him to take a seat.

He had to wait for thirty minutes, trying not to close his eyes. At last a man dressed in a T-shirt and jeans invited him into the interview room.

Once the introductions were made the interview began.

'So, why are you enlisting in our army, Ivan? I believe you are an Australian and this is not your war.'

'I was born in the Ukraine as was my entire family. We immigrated to Australia over twenty years ago.'

'Why?'

Ivan explained the reason in detail.

'I see you are an architect; you might come in handy to rebuild our country when this bloody war is over.'

'It is my intention to return to my family when we have kicked Putin back to his own country.'

'Yes, family is important.'

'You look a fit young man. Do you have any medical problems?'

'No.'

'Okay. You will be required to undertake a medical examination then you will be able to undertake basic training in England.'

'Why England and not here?'

'The British are our allies and have been training our new recruits since the beginning of the war. They have significant experience in combat, having fought in Afghanistan.'

'I see.'

Within a few days Ivan was flying into Britain with three hundred other recruits. Not all of them were young men.

ENGLAND

Ivan, together with several Ukrainian troops clutches an AR-M9F assault rifle, preparing to storm an enemy trench. Others watch on from the rear as their fellow soldiers army-crawl over the barren terrain, toss projectiles and launch their attack.

This is not Ukraine. It is in northern England.

Britain, Australia, Canada, Denmark, Estonia, Finland, Kosovo, Lithuania, the Netherlands, Norway, Romania, Sweden and New Zealand are all training Ukrainian recruits. Over 51,000 recruits from the Armed Forces of Ukraine (AFU) have been trained.

Hundreds of AFU troops undergo training as part of the training operation at any one time. Each recruit receives a kit allocation worth £4,500 ($5,600) including body armour, a fully stocked battlefield first-aid kit and winter combat clothing. These are topped up with additional items before personnel are deployed back to Ukraine.

For Ivan, this training provides an opportunity for Ukrainian soldiers to train in calm conditions and to build a basic knowledge to take back to Ukraine: 'We share in the experience of foreigners, so we learn something from them, and they learn from us,' he says.

'I've worked with many other nations, currently with Dutch trainers,' Ivan says. 'The way they work – all to a NATO standard.' He adds: 'I've seen increasing time allocated to field, tactical and drone exercises, which is what we need in Ukraine right now.'

After forty-five days of intensive training, Ivan and the other recruits in his group return to Ukraine. Now the real test begins.

Between 200,000 and 250,000 Russian soldiers have died in Ukraine since the conflict began, according to the Centre for Strategic and International Studies, which based its recent analysis on U.S. and British estimates.

This is an indication of Russia's willingness to accept enormous losses.

Ivan was standing guard in the damp cold trench. His orders were to ensure the enemy were not moving in on the Ukrainian front line. He was also given the task of looking out for Russian drone strikes.

His good friend Boris approached Ivan with a hot mug of tea; it was much appreciated by the freezing soldier.

It was while he was sipping his tea that a drone carrying a bomb flew over the trench and dropped its lethal cargo. It was too late to warn his comrades several died instantly including Boris.

Ivan was hit with shrapnel ripping apart his right leg. Medics arrived soon after the blast. They examined the fallen concluding they were all dead.

Ivan was stretched to a helicopter and flown to Kiev where he was admitted into the emergency ward of the Main Military Hospital. He had lost a lot of blood therefor the doctors decided to operate immediately.

The operation took four hours Ivan had the leg amputated above the knee.

He came to as a nurse was taking his blood pressure.

'Where am I?'

'"You're in The Military Hospital Ivan.'

'How do you know my name nurse'?

'It's written on your wrist band and on the white board above your bed.'

'So why am I here, I don't remember anything.'

'You were seriously wounded by a Russian drone attack.'

'So, where exactly am I wounded?'

'Ivan I'm sorry to inform you that you have lost half your right leg.'

'Oh shit.'

'Don't worry while you are here with us you will be taught to walk with a prosthetic leg. I don't expect you will be playing football but you will be able walk almost normally.'

Every day a physiotherapist worked with Ivan.

Ivan, once your prosthetic leg is ready, it needs to be fitted properly. The prosthetist will ensure that the socket is comfortable and provides a secure fit.

During the initial fitting, the prosthetist may make small adjustments to ensure the leg feels comfortable and functions well. You'll probably need to wear the prosthetic for short periods at first, to allow your body to get used to it.

Ivan, at the beginning, wearing a prosthetic may feel awkward. It might feel heavy or unbalanced as you move. For the first few days or weeks, you might only use the prosthetic for short periods to get used to the sensation of wearing it. It is essential to listen to your body during this time and take breaks as needed.

A physical therapist will guide you through exercises designed to strengthen the muscles around your residual limb and help improve your balance. These exercises will also help you build the coordination and endurance needed to walk comfortably with your prosthetic leg.

During therapy, you'll start practicing simple movements like standing and balancing on the prosthetic leg, gradually moving on to walking in a controlled environment. Your therapist will provide tips and guidance on how to move efficiently and comfortably. They may also work with you on specific movements, such as walking on different surfaces or climbing stairs.

As you continue your rehabilitation, you'll start to practice walking in different settings. At first, you may only walk a few steps, but as time goes on, you'll start walking longer distances. Practice is key, and the more you practice walking with your prosthetic, the more natural it will feel.

When you first begin walking with a prosthetic leg, you may feel fatigued more quickly than usual. This is normal, as your body needs time to build strength and endurance. As you continue practicing, your stamina will improve, and you'll be able to walk for longer periods without feeling as tired.

Over time, with the help of a prosthetist and physical therapist, you will work on fine-tuning your gait.

Ivan you will be able to lead a normal life.

Ivan's superior office visited him in hospital.

'How are you feeling Ivan? I believe you are walking almost normally.'

'Yes I've got used to it. Are you here to inform me that I will be returning to active duty?'

'No, I'm here to inform you that we are sending you home to Australia. You weren't conscripted you chose to fight Ukraine's enemy and we thank you for it. Thankyou Ivan.'

Ivan boarded a Air France plane and forty two hours later landed in his beloved city.

He entered the arrival terminal and immediately spotted his family Anna was also there waiting to hug her lover.

'You look wonderful his father said.'

'Well, after forty Two hours flying I don't feel wonderful Dad.'

'Let's get you home your bedroom is exactly as you left it.'

Ivan rested up for a few weeks and then decided to seek a position with an architectural firm. He was interviewed by Wolf Architecture and offered a position.

Six months later he and Anna were married two years later Anna gave birth to a baby girl. The following year she gave birth to a baby boy.

Five years on Ivan was appointed a partner in the firm.

PUTIN'S ARMY

CHAPTER 15

This is a Russian soldier's account of his time in the Russian army fighting Ukraine. His name has been changed to Alexi, so Putin doesn't murder him.

On ending up in the war

I volunteered to join the Russian army in August 2022 and signed a short-term contract. In the end, I served for almost a year: 11 months— seven of which I spent in combat positions, where the enemy was always close, and the constant shelling was unimaginable.

I didn't go to war for any ideological reasons; I'd just wanted to see military action since I was a kid. I grew up on cool books about Special Forces and war, and I wanted to experience it firsthand. If someone was boasting about his own exploits, I could say, 'Listen comrade, why are you telling me? I've seen it all too.'

I knew this war had started all because Putin, the ultimate egotist who had delusions of grandeur and had the vision of becoming emperor of Russia and Eastern Europe.

You might wonder how I can call myself a liberal and still go to war, how it fits with my views. But 99 percent of the people I was with were volunteers, and they easily called Putin a fucking idiot.

I knew that the Russian army was fairly incompetent, but at the time, I thought that once there was military action, once there was mobilisation, things would somehow improve. It turned out that the Defence Ministry boasted of how powerful and well trained the Russian Army was. In actual fact it was more like Dad's Army.

As a raw recruit I got two weeks training before they sent me to the front. This was much less than the enemy received. I did have some theoretical knowledge: I'd read manuals, studied mine warfare operations, how to shoot, how to dig trenches. One day, the commander asked me, 'You say you weren't in the army, so how do you know about explosives?'

'Well, you can read about it on the Internet.'

The main stuff, about various weapon types, I learned from the Ukrainian Azov YouTube channel; they explained everything very well, and they had instructional materials. There's nothing like that on Russian YouTube.

On September 2, we crossed the border into Ukraine and immediately ended up near Kherson.

When we got there, the commander asked us, 'I hope you brought your sleeping bags? If you didn't you will freeze your balls off. Alexi looked at his companion's. 'I think we are in for a rough night lads. Surely the army would have supplied them' said Alexi.'

'No they do supply you with a uniform and a gun, that's it.' I replied.

We were instructed to line up to receive our battle jackets.. At least Putin provided us with them however they were XXL size, way to big for your average soldier.

They did come in handy to provide some warmth as my five comrades and I huddled up together.

Alexi was afraid that the world's second biggest army couldn't provide proper equipment. He hoped they would receive adequate ammunition or would they resort to throwing rocks and using sharp sticks when they attacked the enemy's trenches.

On losses from friendly fire

The first death I saw was that of my good friend, Andrii who arrived with me. — And he was killed by our own.

Andrii and I were members of a platoon attacking a Ukrainian trench but we suffered significant casualties. Fortunately, he and I escaped unscathed. We were returning to our line in the half-light when the Russian guard mistook Andrii for a Ukrainian soldier and opened fire. He died right in front of me. I think of my friend constantly.

There was also a guy who had just arrived from basic training who had just joined us at the front. He asked me how to fire a grenade launcher.

He eventually fired it, the blast ripped his arm off, and he died.

At one point, our fellow soldiers were throwing grenades nearby, and the fragments were flying into our dugout, into our observation post. Some of us became victims of friendly fire. Not too bloody friendly if you ask me.

There was one sniper who came to us and said, 'I'm turning 24 today. My ambition is to kill 24 khokhols [a derogatory Russian term for Ukrainians].'

Somehow the Ukrainians discovered the sniper was in our trench. They bombarded us with mortars and their artillery had our range. Many were killed that day. Ironically the sniper survived, as did I. The bastard brought it on us.

On retreating from the Dnipro River's western bank

We stayed on the Kherson front until November in autumn 2022; Our Russian forces withdrew from the western bank of the Dnipro River after a major Ukrainian offensive. We were some of the last to leave the western bank. Were we retreating? Of course we were really running away. They announced that we were "regrouping." We were relieved to finally get out of that hell hole. We were already exhausted after a month and a half there, and they couldn't deliver any ammunition to us because all the bridges and pontoons were being shelled.

During the retreat, we lost equipment, although Russia's Defence Ministry denied this. We actually destroyed it ourselves so the enemy couldn't get hold of it. They did manage to capture some heavy equipment.

Then, they transferred us to the Luhansk region.

My contract expired in December. When I went to find out what was happening with my discharge, the commander started berating me.

'What leave? What discharge? Go fight, you son of a bitch.'

102

I was so disgusted by this inhumane treatment that I just went into the woods without a sleeping bag, bought some vodka, and spent two nights out there. That's when I started having thoughts:

I'll go on leave and never return. I'd rather live in the woods, dig a shelter; it's nothing new to me.

The fear I had was if I got caught I would be thrown into a punishment pit, not a nice place to be.

An internal military police force developed made up of servicemen who regulated everything. In war, there are always those rat-like people who know that if they do whatever the commander says, they'll get privileges for it. They'd run to get food for the officers. Some officers shit in buckets in the dugouts, and they'd carry it out. They beat people and tied them to trees. One of these guys was in charge of this pit, and he would throw anyone disobedient into the pit. Soldiers were severely beaten. My good friend Anton was badly beaten. He ended up there because he started protesting. He'd served for over a year and had never been granted leave. After all of this, he became disillusioned.

They'd throw a grenade fuse into the pit — it's what you screw into a grenade, it makes a loud bang similar to a firecracker. But if you're in the pit, it's very scary: you're already beaten and mentally broken.

These bastards are supposedly on our side. I'm sure the Ukrainians treat their soldiers better than these so-called Russian soldiers.

On spending a year at war

When I first got my leave, I decided to make a run for it and left the country through the forest with the help of an organization, "Go by the Forest" that helps Russians avoid participating in the war. The main reason I absconded was because of the inhumane treatment from the leadership. The second reason was that I'd been under artillery fire for 11 months, and while I'd stayed alive and intact with just a couple of concussions, I understood that my luck might run out one day as it had for so many of my comrades in arms. And the third reason was that I realised that the war was going south. Putin's dream of a reunited Russia had become a nightmare.

"Go by the Forest" provided me with a psychologist, and things got easier. I've come to terms with it: I wanted to experience war, and I got to, so there's no need to cry about it. I've always had this attitude about it: I went there myself, signed the contract myself, and got myself into this situation. I understand it's different for draftees — they were sitting at home, eating pizza, got a summons, and were sent to the front, so I feel sorry for them. But I chose this myself.

I hope Putin makes the decision to end this war.

He could retire to live in his modest 74sqm apartment in Moscow and survive on a modest pension. However I did some research on our illustrious leader.

Putin insists he earns just $140,000 a year as president, lives in a modest and poky 74 sq. apartments in central Moscow and has few other assets.

However I did some research using Google. It's not hard to discover his true wealth.

According to reports, the dictator owns a fleet of luxury cars and dozens of luxurious jets even more opulent than Donald Trump's.

Adding to his luxury arsenal are palatial mega yachts, including one worth $900 million and a high-end watch collection worth millions— all part of his retirement plan.

And then there are his holiday shacks.

This palace is only one of many and I put my life on the line for this bastard. Stupid me.

A LIVING HELL

CHAPTER 16

When Viktor first arrived on the front line, he could see thickets of oak and birch trees from his trench. Months of incessant Russian shelling have since transformed his view into a tangle of charred stumps.

The artillery fire begins just before dawn. A soldier steps into a darkened trench and lights a cigarette, carefully cupping the flame with his free hand. A boom and crackle of outgoing fire sound in the distance.

Viktor, the infantryman, ducks his head under a canopy of camouflage netting and looks up at the brightening sky. The incessant buzz of a drone sounds overhead, moving a dozen metres from one end of the trench to linger just above him.

A moment later, the buzzing sound moves on.

'One of ours,' the 37-year-old soldier says, bringing the cigarette back up to his lips.

The sun finally rises, and the noise of war picks up. For weeks, Viktor has barely slept as Russian drones and artillery continually target his position. During the day, he watches for any attempts by Russian troops to cross a minefield that separates the two sides. At night, he picks up a shovel to dig and fortify his trench.

'They're constantly firing, constantly probing,' he says. 'We have to survive somehow, and we have to hold the line.'

It is the start of another draining day on Ukraine's eastern front line. Monitoring his scratchy radio, Viktor will try to move as little as possible in trench less than 800 metres from where Russian soldiers are amassed. For seven months, Viktor's unit has held this sector of the front, repelling a relentless onslaught of Russian assaults.

Now in the third year of full-scale war, Ukraine's top military leaders openly admit that the battlefield situation on the eastern front has deteriorated. Two years of war have sapped Ukraine's ammunition and manpower, while the country's failed counter-offensive last year sank morale.

As Reuters travelled along the eastern stretch of Ukraine's 1,000-kilometre front line in April, soldiers in infantry, artillery and drone units all expressed exhaustion. They spoke of an acute shortage of ammunition and an urgent need to replenish troops. A new push by Moscow earlier this month near Kharkiv, Ukraine's second-largest city, is likely to further divert precious ammunition and personnel from other sections of the front, stretching Kyiv's military thin at a critical moment in the war.

'Death can come at any moment. I'm starting to get used to the idea of death... that it can happen you can't escape it. In April, analysts say that a severe worldwide shortage of artillery shells means Ukraine will likely be outgunned by Russia for the remainder of the year as Kyiv's allies ramp up production. Analysts could not independently establish how much of the new US weaponry has made it to the front line.

Ukraine's President Volodymyr Zelensky said recently there were no reports of artillery shortages. However supplies were slow. Donald Trump has questioned American military aid to Ukraine many Ukrainians fear the continued support of their most powerful ally hangs in the balance.

Russia, meanwhile, has continued to batter Ukraine with seemingly endless resources.

President Vladimir Putin, riding high as he begins his fifth term, has redoubled his war effort. In 2014, Russian-backed separatists staged a battle to control the Donetsk and Luhansk regions of Ukraine. Since 2022, Putin has made clear his aims to annex the entirety of the area, known as Donbas. To that end, Russian forces have made steady advances in recent months. In February, they captured the eastern city of Avdiivka.

Now, Russia is trying to seize Chasiv Yar, a strategic hilltop city that, if captured, would allow its troops to advance more easily towards the remaining cities of the Donetsk region. Russia's recent incursions in Kharkiv have distracted the world's attention from the heavy battles being waged in the Donetsk region, Zelensky told Reuters.

The Ukrainian armed forces and the Russian defence ministry did not respond to questions for this story.

In recent months, Russian forces have made modest but steady gains along Ukraine's eastern front.

Before Russia launched its full-scale invasion two years ago, Viktor, the infantryman, was working as a window framer outside of Uman, a city in central Ukraine. His wife had just given birth to a baby daughter. They lived with his parents in his childhood home built on a small hill overlooking verdant forests and fields that changed colour with the seasons. (Like all of the Ukrainians profiled in this report, Viktor asked to be identified by his first name only, in keeping with military protocol.)

Viktor received his mobilisation notice four months after the beginning of the war. He was quickly sent to an area in northern Ukraine that borders Russia to dig trenches and fortifications. Later, he was transferred to Bakhmut in eastern Ukraine, where mercenaries from Russia's Wagner group were fighting to capture the city. Last September, Viktor was handed a Browning machine gun and taught how to clean and maintain the weapon. A week later, he was transferred to the front in Donetsk without having fired a single practice round.

When Viktor's infantry unit first arrived here, thickets of oak and birch trees lined the grassy fields. There were still birds in the trees then and the leaves were just starting to change colour. The soldiers dug trenches into the tough black soil but had no time to cover them with wooden planks before the Russian bombardment started. Through winter, the Russians' near-constant shelling reduced the trees and fields to ashes, leaving only a tangle of charred stumps.

In winter, temperatures in Viktor's trench fell as low as minus 26 degrees Celsius. On warmer days, shin-high water pooled at the bottom of the canal, mixing with the earth to turn into slushy mud, soaking everything. All the while, Russian drones flew overhead, hovering above the open trench and dropping grenades.

At the beginning of this year, Russian forces attempted yet another assault, driving an armoured personnel carrier into a field just metres from Viktor's position. He fired at the vehicle with his machine gun and diverted it to a minefield, where it detonated a mine and exploded.

Several of the Russian soldiers died in their vehicle, say Viktor and his commander. Others survived with serious injuries and tried to crawl through the minefield back towards the Russian positions. One of them, a former convict from Russia's Buryatia region, was taken prisoner, Viktor says. Immediately afterward, Russian attacks on Viktor's position intensified.

Viktor and his fellow soldiers use red light in their trenches at night to make it difficult for Russian drones prowling the skies to spot them.

'So of course the Russians were angry. They lost equipment, lost people, so of course they started shelling with everything they have,' Viktor says.

In the heat of battle, all you can do is pray, he says. Around his neck, Viktor wears silver medallions of the Virgin Mary and the crucifix. But when the situation is truly dire, he will pray to every god he knows.

After Russia's failed assault, their drones started dropping gas canisters into Viktor's trench. A colourless, odourless gas would quickly fill the trench as Viktor and his partner fumbled in the dark for their gas masks. Coughing and sputtering, Viktor would crawl into a hole dug into the side of the trench just tall enough for him to crouch in and grab his phone. There, using candlelight, he would flick through photos and videos of his now two-year-old daughter on his phone.

The Ukrainian military says Russia has ramped up its use of riot-control chemical agents to clear trenches on the front line. The US State Department says Russia is deploying an agent called chloropicrin against Ukrainian troops, in violation of the international chemical weapons ban. The US allegations were unfounded, the Russian foreign ministry said this month.

When spring finally came, nothing flowered. All Viktor sees now are the outlines of blackened tree trunks on the horizon.

His exhaustion is palpable – the result of months spent holding the line against an enemy with seemingly endless manpower and weaponry. Death and injury are constant, and every day is a reminder of the asymmetry of the war.

A declassified US intelligence report in December assessed that Russia had lost as much as 90% of the personnel it had at the start of the 2022 invasion, with 315,000 soldiers or injured. Despite the losses, Russia is still estimated to have almost 500,000 servicemen in Ukraine, according to Ukraine's military intelligence agency, and has continued to replenish its troops, recruiting heavily from prisons and from the general public. Ukrainian officials say Russia is planning to add another 300,000 soldiers in time for its summer offensive.

Russia's new defence minister said this month there were no plans for a new mass call-up of troops. Russian officials also say Western estimates of Russian losses are inaccurate.

Zelensky recently signed off on a long-debated mobilisation law to bolster Ukraine's armed forces, which number around 800,000. The law, passed in April, lowers the draft age to 25 from 27. The government hasn't said how many new conscripts the law would yield, and how soon they can reinforce the troops already on the front line.

'It's not like how it looks on a map, with all these pretty lines and arrows,' Viktor says. 'I see my friends, what's happened to them, what we're fighting. It's hell. It's worse than hell.'

In February, the constant Russian assaults sleep deprivation, and fear finally got to Viktor. He woke up one morning frozen with terror, physically unable to go to his position.

'I couldn't calm myself down,' he says. 'Not even that I didn't want to go, but I couldn't go. I was physically and mentally tired.'

Viktor was paralysed by anxiety. What if he failed to do his job properly, what if something went wrong with his gun, what if he let down his comrades, whom he calls his 'brothers' and considers his second family?

He shared his concerns with his company commander. Despite a severe shortage of soldiers on the front, the commander gave Viktor a few days of rest and time to talk with a psychologist. That short reprieve saved him and helped reframe his fear of death.

In the past, he used to think of death as a distant possibility. 'But in a war, you're completely unprotected,' he says. 'Death can come at any moment. I'm starting to get used to the idea of death… that it can happen, and you can't escape it.

'The psychologist said that a person who has faith understands that in death the spirit leaves the body and only a shell remains on earth.'

Viktor's ideas are blurrier when it comes to what follows death, but he knows, with certainty, that there is no salvation for the Russian soldiers who marched into Ukraine.

'I think they're churning in hell,' he says.

Viktor's eyes suddenly flick up. The whistle of incoming artillery makes him duck for cover.

'Get in the hole!' he yells, his voice drowned out by a shattering boom as he flattens himself against the dirt floor of the trench. Another whistles, this time closer, then a sound of impact, of metal meeting earth. The dirt walls of the trench vibrate. Then all is quiet for some time.

A little while later, the exhausted voice of a Ukrainian soldier crackles over the radio, asking for help. The soldier's position, a few hundred metres away from Viktor's trench, has been hit by what appear to be Russian suicide drones, which smash into their targets laden with explosives.

'One 200, three 300s,' the soldier says over the radio, using military code: one dead and three wounded.

'What are my instructions?' he asks, panting slightly. The soldier is ordered to hold his position and not attempt to cross the minefield.

'Plus,' he sighs, acknowledging the order.

A few minutes later, the same soldier's voice returns to the radio.

'What are my instructions?' he asks again, audibly out of breath.

'He's concussed,' Viktor says, noting the soldier's confusion and slurred speech, signs of possible head trauma.

He slumps against the white sandbags that line the walls of his trench and takes off his helmet. 'They're not going to be able to rescue them until dark.'

Over the radio, the injured soldiers are told to wait until nightfall – more than eight hours – for a medevac team to extract them. From there they could be taken to a stabilisation point, a medical facility close to the front line where wounded soldiers receive emergency aid. The commander says another group of men will be transported to hold the position at the same time.

'Do not leave your post,' he tells the soldier on the radio, instructing him to drink water and stay awake.

Several more explosions are heard from the injured men's position.

'They're trying to finish them off,' Viktor says, as the radio crackles again with the voice of the soldier. Several more Russian drones are swooping on their position and dropping munitions.

Viktor sits in silence after learning that a comrade at a nearby position was killed by what appeared to be a Russian first-person view, or FPV, drone. Soldiers say Ukraine needs to double or triple the one million FPV drones it plans to produce this year to keep up with Russia.

Viktor takes another drag of his cigarette. He's lost count of the soldiers he's seen injured or killed. There was a cheerful soldier in his twenties he shared a trench with last fall. He was killed in a heavy mortar attack while Viktor was away from the position for a few days of rest.

Asked for the young soldier's name, Viktor hesitates and squeezes his eyes shut.

'I can't even remember,' he says after a pause. 'I can't even remember where he was from.'

More than anything, Viktor wishes he could go home, but he says the chances of another soldier replacing him soon at his front-line position are slim.

The final mobilisation law passed in April did not include a provision in an earlier version that would have rotated out soldiers who had already served 36 months of duty. Ukraine's defence ministry is now considering a new law that will address demobilisation.

Even with the mobilisation push, many young Ukrainian men do not want to be sent to challenging front-line trenches like Viktor's, soldiers and officers in his brigade say.

'No one will trade with us,' Viktor says. 'Who would want to come here?'

So, he stands guard at his Browning, listening and watching. For hours, the radio crackles on as the injured soldiers wait for the skies to darken. Viktor, ever alert in his trench, looks up at the mid-afternoon sky. A deeper buzzing sound can be heard approaching, a sound that resembles a larger drone carrying a heavier payload. The sound comes closer, then hovers, suspended above the trench.

Viktor strained to hear against the noise of the wind. The buzzing moves away, towards the Russian position.

'Ours,' he says.

A few dozen kilometres away in a demolished village in the southern sector of Donetsk region, another soldier stares at a bank of computer monitors in the dark basement of a command observation point. Roman, a 38-year old commander of a fire support platoon, squints at the screens, a cherry-flavoured cigarette hanging from the corner of his mouth. On one screen is a grid of thermal images, including one showing a tree line in his sector of the Donetsk front.

There is no movement. But Roman knows there are Russian dugouts under the trees. He leans back in his leather armchair and scratches behind the ears of his dog, Marcel, a mixed breed he found in the destroyed village. Another soldier, one of the men in Roman's drone unit, coughs in his sleep as he shifts on an army cot set up in the room.

After a childhood friend was killed in the war, Roman had the words 'hate' and 'revenge' tattooed above his knuckles.

Drones have been used in wars before, but their use has exploded in the war in Ukraine. Russian and Ukrainian forces are now racing to develop and deploy a variety of unmanned aerial vehicles, or UAVs, that can carry out precision attacks, destroying everything from dugouts to multi-million-dollar tanks.

Ukrainian soldiers and commanders say aerial vehicles initially gave them an edge over Russia. They now say Moscow is far outpacing their ability to produce them, in particular the lower-cost first-person view drones, or FPVs, which can be laden with explosives and crashed into targets.

Like thousands of other Ukrainians, Roman volunteered to fight in 2022. At the time of Russia's full-scale invasion, he had been living in Marseille, after almost eight years working and living abroad. He grew up in a working-class village outside of Kyiv with a single mother and left Ukraine to search for a better life. In Marseille, he met his French wife, opened a small pizza restaurant with friends, and spent his free time walking his dog and swimming in the brisk waters of the ocean.

'I was really living my dream. It was everything I wanted after struggling for so long,' he says.

When war broke out, his wife and mother begged him not to return to Ukraine. But Roman felt he wouldn't be able to look himself in the mirror if he didn't volunteer. He quickly joined up with Ukraine's police task force, which has fighting units, first heading to the southern Ukrainian cities of Mykolaiv and Kherson before moving to Bakhmut in Donbas.

Roman practises at a shooting range near the front line.

Last year, he was assigned to accompany one of Ukraine's deadliest snipers, Vasya, who has more than 440 kills, according to the press officer of Roman's brigade. Vasya has been given the prestigious 'Hero of Ukraine' title, a presidential award usually bestowed posthumously, although he is still alive. Roman, who has combat lifesaving training, was tasked with protecting Vasya and keeping him alive as they stalked Russian soldiers in the thick of the Kreminna Forest.

In his new role, Roman oversees 32 soldiers in the 58th Motorised Brigade who are fanned out across mortar and drone positions in the Donetsk region.

Roman's war is now waged almost entirely on monitors.

'It looks like a fucking video game,' he says, toggling between the different windows on his screen.

A few kilometres closer to the front, three soldiers in Roman's unit sit in a cramped dugout, waiting for Roman's orders to launch the drone. Denys, a drone pilot and youngest of Roman's platoon at 21, sits in the corner paving as another soldier teases him for being too green and stupid.

'He's senile; don't listen to him,' Denys says, pointing to the older soldier, who is in his 30s. 'They're so desperate for fighters they're recruiting from homes for the elderly.'

The two soldiers banter on. Serhii, their explosives expert, listens to the artillery and other longer-range drone teams. Units like theirs need to sit closer to Russian positions because their reconnaissance drones normally have a shorter range. Day and night the soldiers sit underground, waiting for an order to fly the DJI Mavic, a quad copter that they use to survey the sector and drop bombs on Russian targets.

Roman's voice comes over the speaker of Denys' phone and the men spring into action. Denys balances the drone controller on one leg, while Serhii attaches a freshly charged battery to the Mavic.

Once in the air, the drone sweeps over a field pockmarked by artillery rounds. The soldiers watch its video feed on a small screen. It ascends higher as it flies over two Russian heavy vehicles destroyed by mines. On the horizon, a line of trees appears.

'Denyska, climb higher; you're flying for reconnaissance,' Roman can be heard telling his drone pilot.

'I'm climbing,' Denys says.

'Higher. Fly sideways,' Roman orders.

As the tree line comes closer, Denys scans for movement on a small monitor.

'No, there's nothing,' he says.

'Okay, come back. I'll watch everything on streams,' Roman says, referring to the live feeds from other reconnaissance drones, as he searches for targets.

The next day, one of the reconnaissance flights spots a Russian soldier standing under a thick cover of trees.

'He doesn't see the drone, so he thinks he's safe,' Roman says in his bunker, looking at the Russian man in fatigues on his screen. 'But nobody's safe.'

Mouth still wet from brushing his teeth, the Russian soldier squints as he tries to make out the soft whirring sound. He turns to say something to his partner, and then spots the Ukrainian drone. He dives into a hole under the trees, just as Denys drops a homemade bomb right on top of it.

'Fucking great! Good boy!' Roman exclaims, staring at a plume of dust and smoke rising from the hole.

Denys asks Roman to repeat the praise.

'I told you you're great; do you need anything else?' Roman jokes.

Leaning back in his armchair, Roman taps the tip of an unlit cigarette on the back of the pack. Marcel, the dog, trots over to him to lean against his legs.

'The idea is – let them be scared. We want them to sit in their holes and not even pop their heads up. If any time you see movement you throw something at them, you throw FPV, you fly a drone, you hit them with artillery, you shoot them with a machine gun, they'll be scared even to go to the toilet,' says Roman.

Ukrainian and Russian forces are racing to develop and produce unmanned aerial vehicles, which can target everything from trenches to state-of-the art equipment on the battlefield.

One of the most potent weapons in the war has been a FPV drone. They have made it almost impossible for both Ukrainian and Russian troops to move on the battlefield without being spotted from above.

These drones, which carry explosives, can be guided to target kilometres away, and cost as little as $500 to produce. Russia, like Ukraine, aggressively targets soldiers' positions and equipment with FPVs. Doctors and staff working at medical stabilisation points in Donbas now says most of the battlefield injuries they treat are from such drones.

There are no reliable estimates of how many FPV drones Russia is able to manufacture every month. Ukraine plans to produce a million FPVs this year, but soldiers and commanders in drone units say they need to double or triple this number if they hope to keep up with Russian troops.

To supply Roman's brigade more quickly with drones, former jewellers and mechanics sit in a village house near the front line, soldering parts for FPVs that can immediately be deployed. Brigades also collect downed Russian drones, which are then taken apart and examined by army engineers who are desperate to keep up with the pace of development on the Russian side.

'Our principle is that the enemy should not be fought by a human being,' says Heorhiy, the commander of a drone company.

Roman's phone rings and he picks up, switching to French. His wife is calling from Marseille to ask about Marcel the dog and the vaccinations he will need for a short leave that Roman is planning to France. The couple married just before Roman enlisted to fight, and in his final week in France he drew up a will to make sure she would be taken care of if he died at war.

Like many Ukrainians, one of his best friends from childhood was killed in the fighting two years ago. Afterward, Roman had the words 'hate' and 'revenge' tattooed above his knuckles, a reminder of the emotions that keep him fighting.

But drone warfare, unlike the close-quarter fighting he conducted in the forests, does not always provide the gratification he seeks. Video clips of the bomb drops, often edited by the soldiers themselves with a hip-hop soundtrack and shared on social media, have an artificial, almost unreal quality about them.

'If I see someone is dead, if we've killed someone, I have zero moral satisfaction; it's just like a video game,' Roman says. Often, he wonders what will actually satisfy the anger and sadness that he feels.

'So your friend is gone. How many invaders do you have to kill to avenge him? 10? 100? 1,000? You're not going to get your friend back,' he says.

A caricature of Russian President Vladimir Putin is used as a target at a shooting range in the Donetsk region.

'You always have to keep in mind that someone sees you,' says Roman.

Soldiers in Ukraine clearly delineate life before and after the war.

Even Roman, who has a background in martial arts and easily fits his new role of commander, never dreamed of becoming a soldier. A look at his social media photos from just a few years ago reveals a different man: carefree and smiling on a messenger bike, eating pizza with his friends, posing in a rice paddy in Bali.

Another soldier describes that sense of disconnection as missing the person you once were and not recognising the new person you've become. When there's a lull in his work, Roman lingers on such thoughts.

'My wife is constantly asking, 'When is it going to be over?' And I say I don't have a fucking answer,' he says. At first, he thought he might be away from home for a year or two. Now, he thinks the war will continue for at least a few more years.

Though he's not interested in demobilising and leaving his men behind, Roman agrees that Ukraine needs a way to help fighters rest. Some of Ukraine's most motivated men and women were the first to volunteer in 2022. Now, so many of them are dead, injured, or exhausted. It's not enough just to draft more people to take their place, Roman says; they need to be properly prepared and trained.

'You can't keep the same people constantly on the front line.'

But the decision of Ukrainians like him to continue fighting isn't really a choice, he says. It's a question of life or death for his people and his country. And if Russia prevails in Ukraine, he's convinced no one in Europe will be safe.

'For Europe and the whole world, we're on the front lines defending it,' Roman says. 'Because this motherfucker will never stop just in Ukraine,' he adds, referring to Putin. 'If you let him get away with it, he's not going to stop over here.'

In an area north of Roman's command centre, artillery units defending Ukraine's eastern front waited for new deliveries of ammunition to arrive.

Ukraine's shortage of artillery shells has become a decisive factor in its struggle to repel Russian advances. Russia's new offensive outside of Kharkiv in north-eastern Ukraine is likely to put further strain along the eastern front, where artillery units have been carefully prioritising targets and rationing shells. In an April interview, Zelensky said that Russia was firing shells at a ratio of 10 to one to those of Ukraine.

Smoke lingers in the air after Ukraine's 57th Motorized Brigade operating near the city of Kupiansk fires shells from a howitzer at a Russian position.

Ukrainian serviceman Oleksii, a soldier in an artillery unit of the 57th, blocks his ear as a howitzer fires at a Russian position. While one artillery installation could fire as many as 100 shells a day in 2022, it was down to as few as two or three a day in April, he said.

One of Russia's targets is Kupiansk, a north-eastern city in the Kharkiv region that was captured by Russia in early 2022 and retaken by Ukrainians later that year. Today, Russian forces are about 10 kilometres away. Oleksii, a soldier in an artillery unit in the 57th Motorized Brigade, is preparing to return to his position in the city after spending a few days resting in a nearby village house.

Oleksii, 27, volunteered to fight five years ago after Russia's 2014 annexation of Crimea. Since then, the town in the Zaporizhzhia region where he grew up has been reduced to rubble. His comrades are all motivated and want to fight, he says, but their biggest concern is the acute shortage of shells.

'When you work and when you have enough shells, you can work and you understand you are destroying the enemy,' Oleksii says. In 2022, one artillery installation could fire 40, up to 100 shells a day. Now, the number has been reduced to two or three shells a day, maybe a dozen on a busy day, he says.

A howitzer of Ukraine's 57th Motorized Brigade fires in the direction of Russian positions in April. Ukraine's President Volodymyr Zelensky has said that Russia is firing shells at a ratio of 10 to 1 to those of Ukraine.

A soldier in Ukraine's 57th carries a shell for a howitzer at an artillery position outside Kupiansk.

In February, Zelensky said Ukraine had received just 30% of the one million shells the European Union promised to deliver by March. The European Commission did not respond to questions about the shell delivery.

By the time Oleksii arrives at one of the brigade's artillery positions, a spring storm has started. Rain is falling and thunder cracks overhead. The hulking 2S1 Gvozdika, a self-propelled howitzer, sits hidden under a cluster of branches and khaki netting, while soldiers take shelter in a dugout nearby.

The unit commander, a slim man with dark hair named Yurii, boils water on a camping stove as his men wait for an order to fire on a column of Russian infantry.

Stirring a cup of tea, one of the soldiers says the months-long shell shortages have made Ukrainian forces on the front lines exceedingly vulnerable. Without shells, artillery units like theirs are unable to cover for infantry on the front lines.

Yurii as the commander of an artillery unit, waits with his team for a fire order in a dugout near the front line. If the US Congress had passed the aid package for Ukraine sooner, he says, the Russians 'wouldn't have taken so many villages and we wouldn't have to fight to take back these villages.'

Russians have factories across their country where they can produce all manner of weapons and ammunition, Yurii says, while Ukraine is largely reliant on the goodwill of Europe and the United States.

'Russians can shoot their artillery like a machine gun,' the commander says. 'It's endless.'

As the wind picks up outside, the men argue over the US election in November and what Trump's possible return would mean for the war.

'But he won't win!' exclaims one of the soldiers.

'Even if he did, he'll still have to help Ukraine,' another says. 'When he's president he won't be able to ignore the opinions of his people.'

Trump campaign spokesman Steven Cheung told Reuters that the former president would make negotiating an end to the war 'a top priority' in a second term, and that European nations need to pay 'more of the cost of the conflict.'

'We are battling an enemy that wants to not only take our territory but to wipe us out,' says a soldier who goes by his call sign, 'Huntsman.'

The problem, Yurii says, is that even after all of the horrors of the past two years of war, there are still so many people in Europe and the US who do not accept all that Putin and the Russian military are capable of.

The horrific images of civilians slaughtered in Bucha after its occupation, the pulverised cities of Mariupol and Bakhmut, the tens of thousands killed, the endless portraits of dead Ukrainian soldiers shared on Facebook and Instagram, the never-ending funeral processions for fathers and brothers, the videos of children draped over their coffins...

'It's not possible, I guess, just by looking at the photos to comprehend the horrors of this war,' Yurii says.

But Oleksii, the soldier in the artillery unit, says Ukrainians have little choice but to keep fighting.

'For our entire history we've been fighting,' he says, rubbing the dust out of his eyes.

The men fall quiet. They sit side by side on narrow military cots, taking sips from their cups. Suddenly, the radio comes alive with an order. The soldiers dash out of their dugout and prepare to fire.

Life as a civilian in Kiev

Borysko was at home in Kyiv it was not an easy time. The Russian attacks on the city are more deadly than ever, and the frequency has also increased. There was one night when Borysko and his family got out of the bomb shelter at 5 am. It was a Wednesday night and the strike on Ukraine's capital lasted 10 hours. There were over 600 drones and over a dozen ballistic missiles that Russia sent to Kyiv to terrorise the city that one night. And the night was just as intense.

Russian Drone

Kiev is being destroyed

Everyone is constantly exhausted, and this is pure terrorism. From my perspective the world has forgotten about this tragedy. And maybe that is just how life is. Everyone has their own problems to deal with. But if Ukraine falls it will have a big effect on everyone. The dictators of the world will start making moves. And the global world order will become more fractured. Also, supermarket prices will go up, as Ukraine is a major food contributor globally, amongst other things.

If you look at the statistics that are published every week, the latest figures estimate that over 1,050,000 Russian soldiers have been killed or injured since the start of their full-scale invasion. This is a huge number. But Putin doesn't seem to care. He will not stop, unless he is stopped. This I believe more than ever. The view in Ukraine is that Putin will try and attack one of the Baltic countries next, probably Estonia or Poland. He will see how far he can push the West. I don't believe Trump will come to Estonia's aid if Russia attacks them. And at that point NATO is then truly a thing of the past. These are dangerous times, in my view.

In Ukraine life goes on, bombs and all. As someone said to me, 'We want to keep living. But not in bomb shelters.' It is often surreal and very hard to comprehend. You can be sitting in a cool, trendy eating spot, having a gourmet pizza, and the next minute an air raid siren goes off, and the vibe changes.

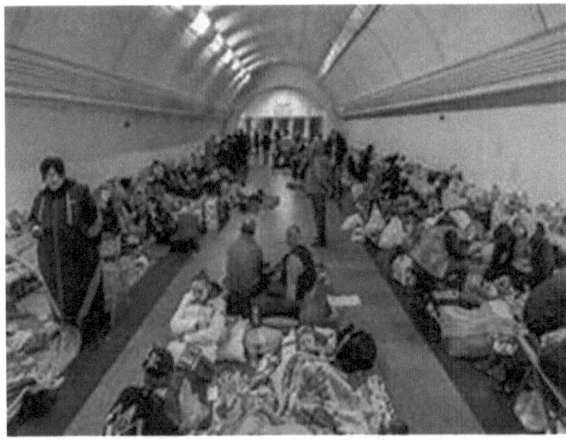

The full-scale war is in its fourth year and there is no end in sight. Most now believe that it will only end when Putin dies, and even then, no one is sure it will then end. This is not Putin's war. This is a Russian invasion.

In Kyiv the mood is low. Everyone is so tired, and anxious. No one can plan a future in this current state.

Half way through the war, towards the autumn of 2023 there was optimism in Ukraine. You could feel the spirit wherever you turned. There was the anticipated counter-offensive, the attacks on Ukrainian cities were not as vicious or as often, and whoever wanted to volunteer to go to the army did so. In the autumn of 2023 there was this thinking that the war was a temporary thing. And now we can see it is a permanent thing. There seems to be no vision now – just a big deadly grind that will go on for years.

By 2024 the mood had changed a lot. The counter-offensive of the previous year did not yield the results everyone had hoped for. Russia started to hit the electrical and heating infrastructure of Ukraine. And the Ukrainian military went on a big recruitment drive with new mobilisation laws coming into effect.

Female Recruits

Then the promised American aid was stalled by over 7 months, and when Trump was elected as the president of America towards the end of that year, the mood hit an all-time low. Trump has not been good to Ukraine, but everyone lives in hope. Perhaps now Trump will finally put some real pressure on Putin.

Conflict

Best Mates

No one believes this will happen though. Trump is making a lot of encouraging noises in the media of late, but most people don't have faith that Trump will actually do something to make Putin's life more difficult.

Now in the second half of 2025 life still goes on in Ukraine, but people are struggling more than ever. Alcoholism, smoking and online gambling are on the rise. Divorce rates are sky high. Trauma is everywhere. You see amputees in the city. Not a lot, but enough to notice.

The number will keep rising. The economy is tight, and nothing is easy or simple. And of course, people are dying. Innocent people are being hit by missiles and drones just about every other night. Then there is also the destruction. If a dozen people die during a night in a Ukrainian city then that is terrible. But what we don't read about in the news are the hundreds more that lost their homes during an evening strike. What happens to all these people? So many families have lost everything. And this terror does not stop. Day after day. Night after night.

The thing about Ukraine, and Kyiv specifically, is that it is so soulful. With so much creative spirit, talent, beauty and inspiration. Why would anyone want to destroy this magical city?! It is all so hard to believe. I have such a love for this city and what it represents.

Before and after Russian renovations

WHO TURNED THE LIGHTS OUT?

WILL THIS BE THE NEXT WAR?

CHAPTER 17

Engineers have discovered 'kill switches' embedded in Chinese-manufactured parts on American solar farms, raising fears Beijing could manipulate supplies or physically destroy grids across the US, UK, Europe and Australasia.

Energy officials are assessing the risks posed by small communication devices in power inverters; an integral component of renewable energy systems that connects them to the power grid.

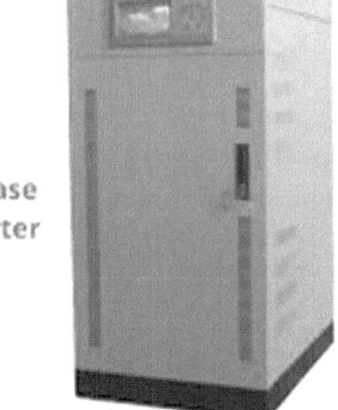

3 Phase
inverter

ML30KW-60KW

While inverters are built to allow remote access for updates and maintenance, the utility companies using them typically install firewalls to prevent direct communication back to China.

But rogue communication devices not listed in product documents have been found in some solar power inverters by US experts who strip equipment hooked to grids to check for security issues, two sources confirmed.

Using these devices to skirt firewalls and switch off inverters remotely, or to change their settings, could destabilise power grids, damage energy infrastructure and trigger widespread blackouts.

'That effectively means there is a built-in way to physically destroy the grid,' one expert declared.

The discovery has raised fears Beijing may maintain the capability to wreak havoc on power grids across the Western world, such is the reliance of renewable energy systems on Chinese-manufactured parts.

British solar panels use parts manufactured in a variety of countries, including China.

It is not known whether the Chinese 'kill switches' are present in any power converters installed on UK wind or solar farms.

Shadow Energy Minister Andrew Bowie called on Labour's Secretary for Energy Security and Net Zero Ed Miliband to carry out an 'immediate pause and review' of its efforts to transition to green power.

The existence of the rogue devices had not previously been reported, and the US government has not publicly acknowledged the discoveries.

Over the past nine months undocumented communication devices, including cellular radios, have also been found in batteries from multiple Chinese suppliers, one of the sources said.

'We know that China believes there is value in placing at least some elements of our core infrastructure at risk of destruction or disruption,' said Mike Rogers, a former director of the US National Security Agency.

'I think that the Chinese are, in part, hoping that the widespread use of inverters limits the options that the West has to deal with the security issue.'

Asked for comment, the US Department of Energy said it continually assesses risk associated with emerging technologies and that there were significant challenges with manufacturers disclosing and documenting functionalities.

'While this functionality may not have malicious intent, it is critical for those procuring to have a full understanding of the capabilities of the products received,' a spokesman said.

A spokesman for the Chinese embassy in Washington said: 'We oppose the generalisation of the concept of national security, distorting and smearing China's infrastructure achievements.'

Meanwhile, the UK Government is conducting a review of Chinese renewable energy technology in the energy system but is still pressing ahead with its efforts to transition from fossil fuels.

Shadow Energy Minister Andrew Bowie told a newspaper yesterday: 'We were already aware of concerns being raised by the Ministry of Defence and the security and intelligence services surrounding possible monitoring technology on Chinese-built wind turbines.

The Australian Minister for Climate Change and Energy Chris Bowen has not acknowledged the threat. No surprise there!

It comes as Energy Minister Bowen pledged earlier this week to put solar panels on 'every possible rooftop right across the country'.

Australia has the most rooftop solar installations per capita globally. It was an Australian scientist Prof Martin Green who invented the solar panel in 1974.

The Government announced plans to create 'solar carports' earlier this month, with supermarkets, offices and shopping centres needing to install solar panels over their car parks.

House builders will also be forced to fit solar panels to all new properties by 2027, under Government plans.

Chinese dominance in the manufacturing of renewable energy technology - particularly power inverters - is stark.

Huawei is the world's largest supplier of inverters, accounting for 29 per cent of shipments globally in 2022, followed by Chinese peers Sungrow and Ginlong Solis, according to consultancy Wood Mackenzie.

Huawei and Sungrow together were reportedly responsible for manufacturing more than half of the world's power inverters in 2023.

Since 2019, the US has restricted Huawei's access to technology - accusing the company of activities contrary to national security, which Huawei denies.

'Ten years ago, if you switched off the Chinese inverters, it would not have caused a dramatic thing to happen to European grids, but now the critical mass is much larger.

'China's dominance is becoming a bigger issue because of the growing renewables capacity on Western grids and the increased likelihood of a prolonged and serious confrontation between China and the West,'

The War to End All Wars

H G Wells

I don't think so

Chapter 18

LIST OF COUNTRIES CURRENTLY AT WAR (2025)

It's Happened Again and Again

Ukraine

Conflict Type: War with Russia
Details: The Russia-Ukraine war continues with major impacts on global geopolitics, energy, and human rights. The frontlines have shifted multiple times, and civilian areas are frequently caught in the crossfire.

Israel & Palestine

Conflict Type: Armed clashes
Details: The Israel-Gaza conflict has escalated since late 2023. Thousands of civilians have been displaced, and the humanitarian situation in Gaza remains critical.

Syria

Conflict Type: Civil war
Details: Over a decade of civil war has left Syria divided. Government forces, rebel groups, and foreign militias still clash in key regions.

Sudan

Conflict Type: Civil war

Details: The conflict between the Sudanese army and the Rapid Support Forces (RSF) has intensified, leading to a major humanitarian crisis.

Yemen

Conflict Type: Civil war

Details: Yemen's war continues between the Houthi rebels and the Saudi-backed government. Starvation and disease have worsened the crisis.

Myanmar

Conflict Type: Military vs. resistance groups

Details: Since the 2021 military coup, Myanmar has been in chaos. Ethnic militias and a civilian resistance movement continue to fight the junta.

Ethiopia

Conflict Type: Ethnic conflict

Details: Despite a ceasefire in Tigray, violence persists in other parts of Ethiopia, particularly Oromia and Amhara regions.

DR Congo

Conflict Type: Armed insurgency

Details: Rebel groups like the M23 continue fighting the Congolese army. Civilians in the eastern provinces face regular attacks.

Mali

Conflict Type: Terrorist insurgency

Details: Mali's northern and central regions remain under threat from jihadist groups linked to ISIS and al-Qaeda.

Somalia

Conflict Type: Insurgency

Details: Al-Shabaab militants are still active across Somalia, especially in rural areas. The Somali government relies heavily on international support.

GIVE PEACE A CHANCE

JOHN LENNON

IS GLOBAL PEACE POSSIBLE?

Peace isn't out of reach. Many organisations and peacekeepers are working tirelessly to mediate conflicts and support recovery. However, lasting peace needs:

- Political reform
- Fair resource distribution
- International cooperation
- Local reconciliation efforts

While parts of the world enjoy stability, millions continue to live under the threat of violence. Understanding these global conflicts is the first step toward advocating for peace and supporting those in need.

The End